Sophia May Eckley

Minor Chords

Sophia May Eckley

Minor Chords

ISBN/EAN: 9783742814500

Manufactured in Europe, USA, Canada, Australia, Japa

Cover: Foto ©Andreas Hilbeck / pixelio.de

Manufactured and distributed by brebook publishing software
(www.brebook.com)

Sophia May Eckley

Minor Chords

MINOR CHORDS:

BY

SOPHIA MAY ECKLEY.

LONDON:

BELL AND DALDY, YORK STREET.

COVENT GARDEN.

1869.

A DEDICATION.

FRIENDSHIP oft weaves a garland fresh and fair,
   And loves to twine it round some fav'rite shrine,
   Nor dreams of aught to blight, or e'en impair
New buds that with the roses may entwine.
You, Dear, have wander'd with me in these hours,
And many a wild bloom pluck'd from nettle's snare,
Untangling oft a rose from thorns in bowers,
Growing, alas, where all the fairest were.
Unfading may it prove, as friendship's light
Serene, as tender every leaf and spray,
To breathe of many a foreign land and sight,
And many a woodland blossom pass'd away ;
Entwine it round the bells that memory chimes,
Cadences ringing of the sunshine, rain,
Keep it to 'mind thee, too, of seasons, climes,
Life passages in desert, tent, and plain,
Endear'd to both by every claim beloved,
Years could not wither, but perennial proved.

LONDON,
November, 1868.

CONTENTS.

CONTENTS.

b

MINOR CHORDS.

B

PART I.

PRELUDE.

THE swallow wings her southward way,
 Deserted nests on tree-tops sway,
 Autumnal winds blow sharp and drear,
Through aspen, beech, and willow near ;
 Summer's symphony is done,
 Autumn's prelude has begun.

May minstrel Autumn's echoes stir,
From windy courts each chorister,
Or are we too obtuse to hear
The prelude of a dying year ?
 Summer's symphony is done,
 Autumn's prelude has begun.

Can music only wing anew,
From instruments we hear and view,
In worldly crowds, in heat and stir,
Where Fashion flaunts interpreter?
  Summer's symphony is done,
  Autumn's prelude has begun.

Ay, organ, viol, harp, may lure
To melodies far more obscure
Than those we find in Nature's spell,
Which only poets love to tell;
  Summer's symphony is done,
  Autumn's prelude has begun.

Then pause, and listen to a strain
That ne'er repeats itself again,
Comes new and glorious year by year,
This prelude of the Autumn's cheer;
  Summer's symphony is done,
  Autumn's prelude has begun.

Seek Nature in her regal hall,
With artists weird and mystical,

Her orchestra so witching, deep,
Her concords that in all things sleep ;
  Summer's symphony is done,
  Autumn's prelude has begun.

PART II.

ATURE'S orchestra is hush'd.
  Life is by the frost-king crush'd,
Mark the leaves' wan carpet meet,
Crumbling underneath our feet.

Winter's ice, and frost, and rain,
Lock the rivulets again ;
Autumn's prelude now is done,
Winter's requiem has begun.

November winds are crying loud,
The brittle leaves weave Autumn's shroud :
Grave Autumn's prelude now is done,
And Winter's requiem has begun.

Low wistful winds that moan the fair,
Wake dying echoes in the air;
Hark, the cadence sadder grows,
Minor in its weary close.

Are our hearts in tune with this?
Or palsied by the world's death-kiss?
Buried in cares, those worldly burrs,
And deaf to God's interpreters?
For Autumn's prelude now is done,
And Winter's requiem has begun.

CHÂTEAULAUDRIN.

TO E. L. G.

"A town in Brittany submerged by the bursting of a lake above it in 1773."—*Les Derniers Brétons, par* EMILE SOUVESTRE.

WHY muse we here, since life has flown,
And death's faint footstep haunts alone
Silent Piazza, vacant street?—
Like rain-drops fall his ghostly feet,
    Through Châteaulaudrin dead!

Muffled the breeze, and dead the air,
And desolate the weed-grown square,
No voice is heard, no human tread,
No light is from the windows shed
    On Châteaulaudrin dead!

Above the city hangs her lake,
Like some dark cloud at point to break
On tile and housetop—so she stood
That morn, ere death's resistless flood
    Left Châteaulaudrin dead.

Thus Naples lies, though not yet cold,
Vesuvius his red torrent roll'd
Up to her gate but yesterday,
Yet Naples sleeps and dreams alway,
    Like Châteaulaudrin dead!

A hundred years have roll'd Time's wheel,
Since life strode here with echoing heel,
And busy traffic drove in haste,
Ere God's hand struck the vineyard waste,
    By Châteaulaudrin dead!

A hundred years, almost, since Fate
Wrote here the city's term and date—
August thirteenth—the numbers see,
Of fatal Seventeen-seventy-three,
    For Châteaulaudrin dead!

The square that night was all alight,
Dancing and beauty charm'd the sight,
Brilliant the grand house in the square,
Zélie the beautiful was there—
    Now, Châteaulaudrin—dead!

Music's soft spell entranced the ear,
Gallery, terrace, far and near,
Flutter'd with beauty's life and breath,
Ere young and old went down to death,
    With Châteaulaudrin dead!

Sweet Zélie, in her beauty rare,
Stood, softly shadow'd by her hair,
Her face just lit with tearful gleam,
As though the sad eyes, in a dream,
    Saw Châteaulaudrin dead!

Her girlish robes of holy white—
We seem to see her virgin plight;
She stands before us at this hour,
As if e'en now her beauty's flower
    Lit Châteaulaudrin dead!

And when she cross'd the crowded square,
To seek the shrine to breathe one prayer,
Old women bless'd her, hands upraised,
Nor dream'd, as on her face they gazed,
    Of Châteaulaudrin dead!

That night her cheek paled in the dance,
Her eye flash'd restless, and a glance
Stole to the door—her partner sigh'd,
For Zélie was that night a bride,
          Nor Châteaulaudrin dead.

The thunder mutter'd of her fall,
The lightning fill'd the dazzling hall;
The deep lake in the distance groan'd,
The hoarse pine at the window moan'd—
          " Dead, Châteaulaudrin dead!"

The rattling sleet upon the blind,
The crazy shrieking of the wind,
The deeper voice that rose and fell
With every gust, seem'd this to knell—
          " Dead, Châteaulaudrin dead!"

The dancers paused, their laughter hush'd,
Fresh cheeks grew wan, then wildly flush'd,
And bold hearts falter'd, terror-tamed,
And white prophetic lips proclaim'd—
          " Dead, Châteaulaudrin dead!"

A nearer crash! a louder roar!
The lake had burst from shore to shore,
O'erwhelm'd the town, which in a breath
Gave up its all of life to death,
   Gave Châteaulaudrin—dead!

Chaplets and gauds, and gold brocade,
Corpses and chattels, monk and maid,
Grotesque cadaverous brotherhood,
Floated upon the ghastly flood,
   O'er Châteaulaudrin dead!

But morning broke, the tempest spent,
The sun from out his chamber went,
No funeral face of grief he wore,
Nor veil'd his light, as to deplore
   Old Châteaulaudrin dead!

But here's the church! is this too dead?
The shrine-lamp lights sweet Mary's head,
Yet Death even here, with mocking sign,
Points outward, points from cross to shrine,
   O'er Châteaulaudrin dead!

In honour of the dead burns bright
This vigil flame by day and night;
Frail sunshine sleeps within the choir,
Deserted, like some silent lyre,
  For Châteaulaudrin dead!

And calmly in the chapel's shade
Is carved in stone a sleeping maid,
Her arm flung upward from her pillow,
As if to ward the whelming billow
  From Châteaulaudrin dead!

A rose falls loosely from her hair,
Zélie the beautiful is there,
Her lover kneels beside in stone,
The bride and bridegroom now are one,
  And Châteaulaudrin's dead!

The lake still moans their funeral dirge,
And death still haunts the treacherous verge,
Fear on the place its evil spell
Has cast—'tis vacant, none will dwell
  In Châteaulaudrin dead!

THE VESPER HYMN.

CHURCH OF ARQUES.

OFTLY steals the wandering sunlight
  Through the stainèd oriel pane,
Down upon the altar falling
  Like a soft celestial rain ;
Solemn breathes the strain of organ,
  Swelling in those arches dim,
Till I fancy angels singing
  In the pauses of the hymn.

Softer, softer breathes the organ,
  And those voices on the air,
When the silence of devotion
  Clasps so many souls in prayer ;
Calm of ages softly veiling
  All that venerable fane,   .
Calm of saints long, long departed,
  Seems to rest on us again.

Tapers glow upon the altar,
  Summer lilies waft their prayer
'Mid the clouds of incense floating,
  Trembling in the painted air,—
Upward wreathing, upward mounting,
  Breathing gardens, O how fair!
Garlands dropt from Heaven's own bowers,
  Down upon the perfumed air;

Where the Virgin-Mother, sculptured,
  With the sweet and holy Child,
Stands, hands droop'd in benediction,
  As through ages long she smiled—
Smiled upon the sad and weary,
  Smiled upon the young and fair,
Waiting ever at that altar,
  Hailing thus the suppliant's prayer.

Hark! the choir so softly singing,
  Sweet, the Virgin-Mother's song,
Now the words of deep thanksgiving
  Rise and swell the roof along;

Die away the prayerful voices,
　　Dies the organ's cadence then,
And the solemn benediction
　　Seems to breathe a vast Amen !

OUTSIDE THE CHURCH.

ARQUES.

SUMMER twilight wraps the churchyard,
　　Where the sleeping are at rest,
With the flowers o'er them breathing
　　Of the gardens of the blest.

Ruin'd windows rise majestic,
　　Broken corbels mount the door,
Tufted with the weed and flow'ret—
　　Nature beauty doth restore.

Here in shadows of the turret,
　　On this old and sunken grave,
Find I time this brief half-hour
　　Of the busy twelve to save—

Save for thought to turn life's pages,
    Mystic pages lent to me,
Where in claustral shadows holy,
    I may turn them o'er with Thee.

Here among the dead safe shelter'd
    In the turf the winds have swept,
Where profanes no heedless footstep,
    Dust of those once loved, long wept.

Summer's story in the churchyard,
    Life and death's perpetual theme,
Where the transept's stainèd windows
    Lure the sunlight's transient gleam.

Here I muse on ages vanish'd,
    Here I read life's mystic scroll,
And, 'mid shadows of the churchyard,
    Dream of the undying soul.

These once lived whose graves record them,
    These once loved, but now they rest,
On their graves I sit and ponder,
    " Dust to dust," earth's sole bequest.

Then how brief seems life's short story,
  Yet who knows what joys these knew?
Ages' sleep in hours I ponder,
  On a grave beneath a yew.

THE STAINED CHURCH WINDOW.

HOW brightly glow'd the Autumn sun,
    Through that great window pane,
Streaming down on the altar like
    A rainbow-rill of rain.
The Apostles in their niches,
    And martyr'd saints grew bright,
As radiant shone each garment
    In that celestial light.

I look'd up to the window, as
    The choir softly sang,
And a flood of rainbow colours
    Stream'd through the panes along;

c

And hosts of angels bright and fair,
  Crown'd martyrs robed in white,
Were looking through those window-panes
  With rapture infinite.

Down look'd they all so tenderly,
  Into the transept dim,
And softly join'd the choristers
  In the sweet evening hymn.
Nor did they float from earth away
  As visions always fade,
Leaving a blank reality
  Where Heaven's Light earth array'd.

But fix'd upon the window there,
  Stain'd on the lozenged pane,
Were all these saints and angels fair,
  In that dim hallow'd fane;—
I wonder sometimes, as I look,
  If they will float away
From that old cathedral window
  In the chapel where I pray.

EUTERPÉ.

N the witching of the gloaming,
 When the Spirit Infinite
Drops his solemn benediction
 On the list'ning ear of night;
Whispering through primeval forests,
 Heard above the torrent's din,
Pleading from the silent flowers,
 Comes the list'ning heart to win—
   Sweet Euterpé.

Throws her dreamy mantle round me,
 Drapes me with her fancies fine,
Mocks Thalia and her Idyls,
 Bids me court *her* muse divine;
Breathes her wary flute so coyly,
 Sings a verse which I repeat,
If one lyric she has taught me,
 That alone is true and sweet—
   From Euterpé.

MY LYRE.

ONE day a lyre was given to me
By an angel I met across the sea;
I had heard no music for many a day,
So I took it gladly, and went my way.

Yes, the lyre came from an angel's hand,
'Twas light and fragile, could I withstand
Such a gentle gift on my pilgrim-way?
No, I took it gladly, and dared to play.

I studied it well, and dream'd o'er it much,
Its strings were of gold—how it answer'd my touch!
Its mountings were costly, and chaste as the dew,
There was music within it my heart well knew.

But one day pausing to study it well,
A blemish I saw in the brittle shell,
A crack had been fill'd, though with passing skill,
Yet it answer'd not quite to the finger's will.

But I sat on the grass and tuned the wires,—
How proud I was of my queen of lyres!
It gave such answers in music to me,
Such marvellous strains of rich melody.

We never were parted, my lyre and I,
It swung on my shoulder, or lay close by,
On sweet Tuscan nights when the nightingale
     sang,
We answer'd each other the dark pines among.

Sometimes my angel then touch'd it for me,
When summer's storm smote the great cypress tree,
Drowning the notes of its cadences faint,
With tones like the voice of some pleading saint.

And often the lyre vibrated at will,
When no earthly touches the gold strings might
     thrill,
Wak'ning the chords to a soft reprimand
For my veilèd sense of the near spirit-land.

And oft came the moon with her silvery wings,
Jewell'd the mountings, and finger'd the strings,
Kindled strange music, gave words to the breeze,
And waken'd my lyre to voices like these.

The fountain dripp'd down to its soft minor chord,
And the river too whisper'd his low chiding word,
The nightingale trill'd from the darks of the pine,
And answered my lyre in echoes divine!

    *   *   *   *   *

But alas! every lyre will fall out of tune,
E'en gold strings will snap, either later or soon;
Alas! every song must come to an end,
And Time, that robs blossoms, earth's music may
    rend.

Thus even my lyre proved faithless at last,
In facing a Roman autumnal blast;
Though even an angel had brought it to me,
All at once it lost sweetness, tone and melody.

The crack I saw widen, the music impair,
Nor could earthly fingers the evil repair ;
From each full vibration of tone, true and clear,
Came harshness and discord to jar on mine ear.

To the garden I took it all broken, unstrung,
And down 'mong the roses my lyre I flung,
No longer I loved it as once close by me,
Though I wept for the Past and its rich melody.

I pick'd some green laurel all dripping with dew,
On the dear lyre I threw it, yet too well I knew,
Like my tears, even this would but rust the gold
      strings,
Nor recal the flown Past with its merciless wings.

O well I remember how dawning crept on,
When first I was sure that my day-dream was
      gone
Like mist on the mountain, like dew on the
      flowers—
O what have we here that we dare to call ours ?

Once more though I lifted it wet from the ground,
With horror I started, the mystery found—
In the heart of my lyre, which had once seem'd
    divine,
A snake was coil'd up'in the treacherous shrine.

Yes, there coil'd the snake in the lyre that I loved,
With its venomous sting, its motive I proved—
It had gnaw'd all the strings, it had widen'd the
    seam,
Had ruin'd my instrument, shatter'd my dream.

      *   *   *   *   *

But O ! when the storm of my passion was spent,
At night through the dark to the garden I went,
I lifted my lyre and the broken strings kiss'd,
Then left it in darkness, in rain, and in mist.

MY LUTE, OR COMPENSATION.

FROM the river I came, my hands full of
         reeds,
Of beautiful pebbles, moss, fern, willow seeds,
I long had been trying to catch its low song,
And the prelude it whisper'd, the long reeds among.

I pull'd up the reeds, but the god was not there
To teach me to play, so I took them with care,
And carried them home, but no music I found
Would come from my reeds, not an echo of sound.

But one day I miss'd them, those dear silent reeds,
The moss and bright pebbles, and long willow-seeds,
And close to the shelf where their shadows they
        threw,
Hung a fairy-like lute on a ribbon of blue.

My first thought was sorrow—to leave it and go,
Could I care for this lute, or life's music renew ?
Yet I saw with surprise that the lute had no strings,
So no music could come on melody's wings.

'

But under the ribbon the strings were low laid,
And ere I could mount them, a soft serenade
Breathed from the lute all unstrung as it lay,
A faint prelude first, then a sweet roundelay.

What matter'd the strings then if such strains could
     come
Without even touches, and wing to their home
Unbidden, unpray'd for, this heart for a shrine ?
O music, heart-music ! and yet to be mine.

Not from earth's reeds then life's music I found,
Nor from my own seeking the wide world around,
But infinite love and compassion had given
Compensation for loss, in music from Heaven.

When summer noon glows, how sweet are its
      strains,
Through hoar-frost of winter, and wild beating rains,
It is always in tune, and no discord nor jar
Ever comes from my *lute*, the soul's music to mar.

It plays in the morning soft hymns before light,
Serenades me at evening, brings " songs in the
      night,"
Its notes but grow mellower as earth's hours
      fly,
And O! will be sweeter in Heaven by and by.

But my lyre! my poor lyre! it now sleeps in the
      dust—
How often I muse o'er that day-dream of trust!
And the tears will fall now, as thought brings
      back past hours,
Which memory uproots with a scent of dead
      flowers.

A SOLDIER'S GRAVE.

In memory of Lieut. H. M. B. who died serving his country
in the Battle of the Wilderness, May, 1864.

To M. D. and C. A. M.

IGH in the ranks of the Lord of Hosts,
　　March the soldiers of the Right,
Heroes transplanted by death's stern call,
　　From rebellion, warfare, night.

High in the ranks, not dead are they,
　　Though they fell in the battle morn;
We call them dead, and with martial tread
　　Their bodies to dust are borne.

But safe from the warfare, fury, death,
　　Released from the foe's hot fire,
Safe in the armies of the Lord,
　　They still march higher and higher.

In the shroud of his country's stainless flag,
  With flowers that May has given,
Lay a wreath of bay on this soldier's grave,
  Then follow his steps to Heaven.

And write on the marble that hides his face,
  " He died for his country's glory,"
And leave it to History's page to embalm
  The deeds of this week's sad story.

Though still in the ranks, not dead are they,
  These braves to their country given,
They've but laid down their arms at the gate of
      the King,
  And are taking their rest in Heaven.

ANOTHER SPRING.

ANOTHER Spring,—the robins sing,
  While leaves are wakening to the light,
Morn treads upon night's dusky robes,
  And Spring upon the frosty blight
    Of Winter's long campaign.

Hark! carols loud from leafy shroud,—
  O early Spring and tenderest leaves,
In all your greenery so bright!
  Silence in us the sigh that grieves
    For what could not remain.

O hide the bier,—another year
  Sings new-born life to bud and leaf—
Shall robins sing another Spring,
  And we grow sceptic in belief,
    Or lose our faith in Life?

Life treads upon the robes of death ;
    Death's angel comes, but only wins,
Till dawns the Resurrection morn
    The day when that new life begins,
        The deathless life of love.

Another Spring the angels sing,
    While souls awaken to the light,
Morn treads upon night's dusky robes,
    Eternal Spring on Winter's blight,
        And glorious Day on Night !

GRAVE-ROSES.

A HUNDRED years have swept this grave,
    And only roses left in trust !
But loving hands that planted them
    Have long since crumbled into dust.

None are left this grave to garnish,
　　Nor bid fair Summer's roses blow;
Only this lone one drops her petals
　　Over the grave, like Memory's snow.

Rosy snow-flakes! Death's December,
　　May Heaven's perennial Spring be theirs!
Only to us a wintry churchyard,
　　A lingering rose, and half-breathed prayers.

DREAMS.

 EARLY dreams! sweet spring-tide
　　　　　dreams
　　Of childhood's fleeting hours,
When through youth's wizard glass we gazed,
　　And trod her myrtle bowers.

O Summer dreams, sweet Summer dreams !
   O hope! O trust! O joy!
The faded gleams, the broken links
   Leave gold—but with alloy.

O later days, grey Autumn days!
   Bring riper fruits for wine,
And as earth's dreams prove only dreams,
   Clear Faith begins to shine.

O golden days! eternal days!
   The days that are to come,
When glorified we see His face,
   And call His Presence Home!

II.

ONE half our lives we dream away,
   Another half we sleep,
Night-dreams and day-dreams interweave—
   From sleep we wake to weep—

Day-dreams so subtle, vague, and wild—
  How oft we kiss the chains!
Those chains of slavery fondly link'd,
  So sadly link'd to pains.

But if in dreams we wear away
  The gold of life's best hours,
O let us guard the bloom, at least,
  Of holier, heavenlier flowers.

Some bloom of Heaven kept in the soul,
  Though faint the blossoms seem,
Safe in that shrine where Christ should be
  The soul's one only dream!

TWO CHILDREN.

KNOW a child most wondrous fair,
  With tender eyes and sun-kiss'd hair,
The loving clasp of whose little hand
Seems a new link to the spirit-land.

But I think of another child as fair,
Fairer than this earth's fairest fair,
And one whom an angel came to kiss,
That he might awake in endless bliss,

Where the fadeless days are long and clear,
And blight and frost cannot draw near,
Where even the flowers may never die
In the breath of Immortality.

And I love the child, so wondrous fair,
With his tender eyes, and sun-kiss'd hair,
That dream of Italy that round him clings—
Like a Northern bird on Southern wings.

Then I watch my own as years sweep by,
Growing in grace under God's own eye,
And I marvel to think how I could mourn
When the angel came on that weary morn,

And press'd on his lips that kiss full thrice,
That he might awaken in Paradise,
Whispering, " The angels are calling thee,
To play with them by the crystal sea."

And often I've wiped the tears away,
And tried to fancy him there at play;
But sure I am he is happier far
Than the happiest children round me are.

But I love the child so wondrous fair,
With those gentle eyes, and sun-kiss'd hair,
The dream of Italy that round him clings—
This Northern bird on Southern wings.

And I pray that the angels may guard this flower,
Shield him and train him for that same bower,
So when the angel kisses him thrice,
He too may awaken in Paradise.

WHERE?

 WHERE will the Singers be,
    In the great Beyond, O where?
They who have dropt their lyres crown'd
    With immortal laurels here.

The Singers of every clime,
   The Singers in every key,
The Poets, where then will they meet
   On the banks of Eternity?

Say, will it be under Palms,
   Palms such as they loved to sing,
In scenes more grand, entrancing, fair,
   Than a poet's dream can bring?

And are they now still singing
   Without each whispering lyre?
For they dropt them in the shadows here,
   When they were call'd still higher.

The stately march of Milton,
   His rhythm grave and grand,
Great singer of "Lost Paradise,"
   King of the minstrel band.

And weird, majestic Danté,
   Great Tuscan Poet, he
Who sang of glorious Paradise,
   In marvellous imagery.

And Shakespeare, Shelley, Keats,
　　O mystical array !
Have ye all found that Pierian spring
　　Which rippled to your lay ?

And have ye bathed your lyres
　　In that celestial stream,
To sing your immortality,
　　As ye were wont to dream ?

YEAR AFTER YEAR.

SUMMER days ! O summer days !
　　And are ye really flown ?
Your bloom still lingers on the soul,
　　Though autumn winds will moan—
Will moan as thrill the dying leaves
　　To music as they go,
Whirling and eddying as they reach
　　The Avon's silent flow,
　　　　　　　Year after year.

O Autumn winds! O Autumn winds!
  O silent Avon's flow!
O willows weeping on your brink!
  O Autumn winds that blow!
Year after year, the same refrain,
  Though varied be the key,
Is sung, and no discordant notes
  Mar the sad symphony,—
              Year after year.

Year after year, to greet, to part,
  O Summer days too short!
O Autumn winds! O Avon's stream!
  Of what then your report?
The loaded wains, the harvest ripe,
  The sobbing winds but tell
Of Summer flowers, of Summer fruits,
  That die in each farewell,—
              Year after year.

O Summer days! sweet Summer days!
  Ye are not truly flown,
Your bloom still lingers on the Past,
  Though Autumn winds will moan;

The bloom of Summer in the soul,
　Of holy sweet content,
Immortal bloom—immortal calm,
　In this our banishment,—
　　　　　Year after year.

A DREAM-ROSE.

PLUCK'D a rose, all wet with dew,
　It grew in a garden wild,
And many a nettle wounded me,
　Ere I caught my flower-child.
But I put it in my bosom then,
　And wore it night and day,
And sweet it perfumed all life's hours,
　Ere it wilted quite away.

But one day from the stalk it fell,
　From my bosom to the ground,
Where anyone who chanced to pass,
　Might find the rose I own'd;

But the leaves from which it broke away,
   Still clung to their resting place,
Alas! 'twas a thorn that lurking there,
   Had caught them in the lace.

But when it dropt, some petals fell,
   I pick'd them up all dry,
And press'd them in my heart's lock-book,
   'Tween leaves of Memory;
And when I chance to ope that book,
   And turn the pages o'er,
Faint scent of wither'd petals brings
   Earth's requiem, " Never more ! "

Then all earth's roses seem to bear
   The bloom of the sepulchre,
Vague spectres of those on fadeless shores,
   The perennial "Forever" there !
Dream-roses, all of earth, farewell!
   Ye proved the dreams ye were,
I've long been tired of grasping you,—
   Tired of castles of air.

FLOWERS THE DEAD WEAR.

O, let them rest, for ever rest
  In the coffin round the head—
See! they have scarcely wilted here
  In the winter of the dead.
But softly lift the winding-sheet,
  And in the waxen hand,
Leave this pale Autumn rose to die
  In death's dim frozen land.

He went to sleep thus holding it
  Still tight in his dying grasp,
This rose of life he clung to here,
  Till Death said, " 'Tis my clasp,"
This rose, it seems, was only born
  To trim a shroud of death,
For long it is since Summer kiss'd
  Its petals into breath.

And leave the portrait hanging round
   The shrunken marble neck,
With mocking tress of faded hair,
   A grave-shroud now to deck!
But on the frozen, silent heart
   Which ne'er will beat again,
Lay this heart's-ease so sadly stain'd
   With olden tears of pain.

With flowers dead, with riven vows
   Together let them sleep,
And best of all the love that's dead—
   See, Dear, I do not weep;
For he was false I thought so true—
   For truth I loved him, Dear—
But stay, I have no bitterness,
   He lies too helpless there.

So still and cold, he cannot feel
   How weary life goes on—
So false—cast to the winds are leaves
   On which glad Summer shone;

For on he danced as dead leaves dance,
　　Through life's bewildering plot,
But like dead leaves, his heart at length
　　Got trodden underfoot.

And then he sought this dead rose here,
　　All wither'd, faded, dry,
And blighted as the flowers once press'd
　　'Tween leaves of Memory.
So wrap the winding-sheet close round
　　Love's statue, frozen, dead,
Then take me from the coffin, Sweet,
　　I'm ready now to wed.

VOUÉE AU BLANC.

AND they vow'd her to the Virgin,
　　And they clothed her all in white,
The little Blanche, the lily fair,
　　A blossom of earth's night.

They vow'd her to the Virgin's love,
   On that cold and wintry day,
When Death drew near the cradle-side
   To steal our Blanche away.

And all in white they robed her,
   And then to the Virgin's care
Consign'd the little lily Blanche,
   The fairest of the fair.

And she never wears a colour,
   Save the violet in her eyes,
And rosy hands like little shells
   Just dropp'd from Paradise,

And in the flood of golden hair
   That ripples from her brow,
As if just spun from Heaven's own cloud,
   To consecrate that vow.

Thus they vow'd her to the Virgin,
   That sweet and sunny child—
When grim Death forsook the cradle,
   And sweet Mary on her smiled.

46

IN MEMORIAM.

I.

THE vase is shatter'd, and the lamp is
    spent,
The flame burnt out—O darkness, tears, lament,
Ye can avail not! In those silent halls,
Cold winds her requiem wail, sad Echo calls—
Calls for the song that evermore is hush'd,
Calls for the spirit-flower that death has crush'd,
Calls for one strain of that immortal lyre,
For one more spark of that Promethean fire;—
But Silence weeps her rhythm, voiceless, grand!
And Memory, with her funeral torch, *will* stand
Lighting the labyrinth of a vanish'd Past,
As Love, her eyes still shading, casts one last
Long look, to catch e'en one unfinish'd bar,
One strain of music from *her* home afar.

Florence, *June* 29, 1861.

II.

Though mute her lyra in those haunted halls,
Though Silence weeps, and Echo wildly calls;
Though all Italia's tears dropp'd on those strings,
When came the angel Death and gave her wings—
Dark'ning the windows of a ruin'd home,
The fireless hearth, the vacant chair and room,
Where once had breathed that gentle spirit-flower,
With all its wealth of tenderness and power—
Though dropt her lyra in the shadows here,
It fell not dumb on a forgotten bier;
Immortal laurel blooms round each gold string,
Her music's strains the soft south winds shall
　　sing,
And Love, that counts no change, nor blight, nor
　　death,
Shall sing her deathless fame to latest breath.

OCTAVES.

E

WHISPERS AT FONTAINEBLEAU.

To C. C. AND F. D. P.

HUSH! hush! for the silence is pleading
  In whispers wherever we go,
E'en the leaves have their burden to sing us,
  While dying at sweet Fontainebleau.

As chords in a symphony plaintive,
  Will awaken some sad long-ago,
So the leaves and the silence are laden
  With the secrets of old Fontainebleau.

And the rain too is falling, soft falling
  On the leaves of this mystical score,
With the wind-harp's sad interlude breathing
  Soft cadences faint to restore.

But what are these whispers that follow,
    And haunt us wherever we go ?
Are they hid in the rain-drops, and wind-harp,
    To echo of past Fontainebleau ?

O no ! other phantoms pursue us
    Through the aisles of this forest so vast,
Bid us follow their mournful procession,
    Sing their dirge of the wonderful Past !

Sing of kings, whose bright sceptres are shatter'd,
    And of crowns, now corroded by rust,
Of queens, whose state pageants and sorrows
    Found at length but a pillow of dust !

In the calm of this grand Mausoleum
    Let us wait till the shadows appear,
And watch them so subtly transforming
    The whole to a sepulchre drear.

Gates ope to the spirit of Even,
    Shrines light from the great western fire,
Emblazon'd by jewels of sunset,
    Which flash through the traceried choir.

From this sepulchre phantoms are gliding,
   They are bearing a mystical bier,
While the hearse at a distance is waiting,
   And the death-chant croons low on mine ear.

'Tis the burial of Summer's brief glory,
   'Tis the death of a wonderful year,
A ghostly procession doth follow,
   Strewing wreaths of dead leaves o'er the bier.

And such are the Fontainebleau whispers
   While that bier through the forest is borne,
Fern plumelets from far wave their farewells,
   Dim, rusty, wind-broken, and torn.

But turn we from pageants of glory,
   From Emperors, monarchs, and pride,
To follow the footsteps less fleeting,
   Which are waiting our wanderings to guide

Through the forests of life, though perplexing,
   Through the mazes and copses most deep,
And forget not the endless awaking,
   After Time in his chasm shall sleep ;

To find earth's last forest is skirted,
   The maze of all mazes pass'd through,
Where the poets are wak'ning their lyres
   To a song which for ever is "new."

Then hush! for the silence has pleaded
   Her whispers while onward we go;—
O, we will not forget you, wild echoes
   Of Autumn at sweet Fontainebleau!

September, 1866.

REAL.

 SLUGGISH stream,
   With treacherous brink,
  And slippery hold
   For steps that sink.

Long ragged grass,
   With coarse weeds rank,
Fringing the brink
   And crumbling bank.

And slothful fish,
  That rarely rise
For a floating meal
  Of water-flies.

The peasant hums,
  Her garment wrings
In the eddying tide,
  And careless sings.

To her a stream,
  Or thick or clear,
As floods may swell
  Or drought may sear.

IDEAL.

 POET is musing
      Beside the same stream,
Yet different far
  Is the light of his dream.

The sun has bewitch'd it,
    And wrought a gold link
To chain brim to margin—
    Of what does he think?

That weeds change to flowers,
    And rough pebbles to gems,
And the grass and the dew-drops
    Weave diadems.

There's a moral for verse,
    As each lone grassy spire
Grows upward and onward,
    Still higher and higher.

Is it not then our fault
    If we blindfold will rove
On the banks of Life's river,
    And see not the Love

Which turns night into day,
    Even weeds into flowers,
And from discords brings concords,
    And makes all Nature ours?

" GOLDEN HOURS."

A Picture at the Great Paris Exposition by
F. Leighton, A.R.A.

IN an old Venetian palace
   That standeth in the sea,
Whose steps are wash'd by tuneful chords
   Of wavy minstrelsy ;
In a chamber, ghostly, solemn,
   With arras hung, and quaint
With Albert Durer's carvèd oak,
   And shrine of patron saint,

And oriels looking to the blue,
   The blue of wave and sky,
Like sapphires set with opals, dropt
   By sun-light's fiery eye.
In this dim, deserted chamber,
   The spider swings her loom,
And knots her subtle meshes,
   Sole tenant of the gloom.

In tapestries, all tatter'd, stain'd
 With mildew, damp, and mould,
She spins in th' faded satin, mocks
 The needle-work of gold ;
Stringing the broken lyre too,
 And faded ribbon blue,
And the branch of wither'd willow
 Tied on the silver screw.

Here in its shadowy alcove hangs
 Among the lost and dead,
A wonderful, sweet picture, long
 To dim tradition wed ;
Only a shrunken canvas, which,
 Two hundred years and more,
Has told the same old story, and
 Will tell it o'er and o'er.

The tale of Love, of Faith, of Hope,
 When golden seasons shone,
Ere mocking echoes whisper'd sad—
 Where has the gold all gone ?

No more it shines untarnish'd, bright,
   As in that picture's gleam,
That wizard-picture of those two
   In love's first golden dream.

His hands are wand'ring o'er the keys—
   Unmindful now of all
Save him, she turns her back on life,
   Nor heeds what may befall ;
" Golden hours," by music wing'd,
   Your gold is deftly caught,
He was a poet-painter, who
   This golden vision wrought.

Alas ! I wake from Southern dreams,
   From dreams of Venice bright,
Far from Venetian phantasies,
   And myths of Venice light ;
The palace and the classic sea,
   The haunted chamber lone,
Where *might* have hung this picture fair,
   In golden seasons gone.

My dream grows pale, and in a crowd
　　My fancy wings away,
In a modern gallery I stand,
　　This fair Parisian day ;
But the gold that lights that picture,
　　This fancy lit for me,
Of that old Venetian palace
　　That standeth in the sea.

TWO LANDSCAPES.

 LOOK abroad on this gay, thoughtless
　　scene,
The Tuileries' garden, with its wealth of green,
The youth of new-born Summer on the trees,
As if no blight could ever fall, or breeze
Bring aught but health upon th' elastic air—
This Spring Parisian, transient as 'tis fair ;
The children, too, now mellowing the scene,
Life-flowers of every hue, of every sheen,

And all this life as giddy as if sin
Had never stain'd the world where Christ hath been.
O trace the picture now of inner sight,
Another landscape rises in Faith's light ;—
The world is still as fair, the children in
As sweet unconsciousness of grief or sin,
Responsibility to them unknown,
They only follow where the way is shown ;
But this, the soul's rare picture, seems to me
Imbued with more abiding purity,
For here I mark a landscape swift unroll,
With atmosphere and colours of the soul !
No garish glitter of Parisian day,
No rosy bubbles vanishing away ;
Not like the pageant of a feverish dream,
That, even while discern'd, can only seem,
While pleasure's cup, ambrosial to the sip,
A nectar holds that cloys upon the lip ;
But this, the inner landscape of the soul,
Is calm, serene, God-held—a happier whole !
Here pearly tints of morning, cool and grey,
Invite the angels in their white array ;
And we can sit and wait for them to come,
And feel their shadowy presence in our home !

A FRAGMENT OF HISTORY.

Paris, June 7th, 1867

IN the shadows of the gloaming,
    Ere the spirit of the night
Dropt the dew from Eve's gold chalice
    On the Elysées fading light,
Swept a cortège grand, imposing,
    Life-exciting, near and far,
With the Emperors of two nations—
    Napoleon and the Czar.

Onward moved the brilliant cortège,
    Shielded by the glittering steel,
Waved the plumes of bright battalions,
    Warriors arm'd from head to heel ;
'Mid the pomp and dazzling glory,
    Splendours of a gala day,
Few were dreaming 'mid those thousands
    Death was crouching in the way.

'Mid the strains of martial music,
  Cymbal's clang and clarion's breath,
Came, on shadow-wings of evening,
  Thoughts of Poland, boding death;
Cries from Poland in her anguish,
  Smote upon an exile's ear,
One of thousands there assembled
  Caught the word, the word so dear:—

Poland moaning in her anguish,
  Orphan'd, widow'd, dead, and drear—
'Twas rash, but yet it was for Poland
  That pistol loaded, ball so near;
As the assassin's hand was lifted,
  And the air the bullet cleaved,
The arms of France the deed prevented,
  And the murderer's hope deceived.

Then died the day in clouds and showers,
  In festive scenes, night's masquerades,
Though Poland's tears bedimm'd the banner
  Floating o'er the Elysées' shades.

SILVER ACRES.

 STOOD at my window watching the
      night,
  The night that hung over the sea,
I shall never forget that picture so fair,
  Nor the vision that cheated me.

It was no more a sea I was gazing on,
  But acres of glittering grain,
Which were waving and tossing their jewell'd heads,
  Or bent low by the summer's rain.

And the reapers were wand'ring here and there,
  With sickles of burnish'd gold ;
And children were playing,—moon-gems lit their
      hair,
  Moon-flowers they cull'd in this wold.

And ever and oft their voices came
  Like the rippling of parted waves,
Then clear and ringing, as pebbles sing
  When the last billow over them laves.

Thus deep into night at my window I stood,
 Near those acres of glittering grain,
Still waving and tossing their spangled heads,
 Amid sheaves in the high loaded wain.

At length from my moonlight dream I awoke—
 But where were those acres of grain?
The reapers and children, where then, O where?
 Shall I never behold them again?

For the moon, night's illusive magician had been,
 Had planted this wonderful field,
In her glittering path these acres had sown,
 This harvest of fancy to yield.

Yet often again from that window I've look'd
 For those dream-land acres of grain;
But they're gone—like the fading dreams of our
  youth,
 To return, alas! never again.

F

MY WINTER GARDEN.

TO F. A. E.

FRESH roses, and lilies, and pink im-
     mortelles,
And branches of holly with bright scarlet bells,
Here in their beauty so fresh and so green,
All winter my own living garden have been.

Though not in stiff parterres befringed with the
     grass,
Nor in the green fields where the cool shadows
     pass,
Nor there where the honey-bee seeks her rare bliss
In the 'wildering spell of a sweet blossom-kiss;

But in a Parisian bright drawing-room, hung
With draperies, pictures, and mirrors among,
In a shadowy nook by the warm fireside,
My books and my garden, my joy are and pride.

The little French sparrow sometimes ventures in,
To pick at my greenery from the street din,
For the crumbs that I drop on the broad window
    sill
Oft the dingy pets lure to their shy breakfast still.

But my garden is blooming all fragrant and fair,
And my books seem the happier when *her* flowers
    are there ;
My poets ! life's silver wheat amid the rank tares,
Poor poets ! how little the world for them cares.

They pipe their brief carols, they sing their sad lays
On the bough nearest heaven, and they court not
    earth's praise,
As the nightingales sing because carol they must,
Though the world grovels on in her turmoil and
    dust.

But my garden perennial is blooming and fair,
In spite of the outer world's chill frosty air,
And Love is still dreaming among her thought-
    flowers,
Unguess'd at her joys in calm solitude's hours.

And the gay world below, now in sunshine, now
    mist,
May call us life-dreamers and count us less blest,
While we with our books, and a few wint'ry
    flowers,
Can find an Arcadia in life's darkest hours.

THE STATUE BY THE SEA.

THE LOVER.

ITH hair unkempt, with tearful eyes,
    With kreel upon his shoulder slung,
Low on the golden sands he lies,
    His arms upon the sea-weed flung,—
        Watching.

Wave over wave, each feathery crest
    Nets its foam-meshes on the shore;
How vain, alas! to dream of rest
    Where ocean murmurs " nevermore,"—
        Watching.

The sea-mew swoops above the ledge
　　That half conceals her lonely nest
Of white-wing'd broodlings in the sedge ;
　　Her startled cry invades his rest.—
　　　　　　Watching.

He wakes bewilder'd from his dream,
　　The burden from his shoulders thrown,
The stars from out the wind-cloud gleam,
　　And he stands, dazed with cold—alone—
　　　　　　Watching.

Watching for what ? some boon to gain ?
　　Perchance his ladye-love to see ?
He long an exile,—O the pain !
　　To find her false, or coldly free,—
　　　　　　Not watching.

Or haply find her dead and gone,
　　Or, worse than death, from him estranged,
Hope, flattering whisper'd, Marion,
　　And love like her's has never changed ;—
　　　　　　She's watching.

THE CASTLE.

HIGH on a bold and rocky steep,
　　Where beats the proud rebellious sea,
Raking the pebbles from the deep
　　To hurl them upward scornfully,

A castle stands, now ruin-seal'd,
　　The vines exhausted, and the soil,
Nor corn, nor olive more will yield
　　Their increase to the hireling's toil.

Only the aloes' wrinkled cheek
　　Betrays the scars of centuries fled,
And only one is left to seek
　　For life where Love itself seems dead.

A maiden in that castle dreams,
Her faded hair in moonlight gleams,
The battlements she haunts at night,
And gossips whisper of a knight—
　　　　　　　　Waiting.

An armèd knight, with sword and shield,
And clanging spurs, as from some field
Of death and victory, who had come,
Triumphantly to lead her home,—
       Waiting.

One night,—thus I the legend read,—
The absent lover came indeed;
Long she had plighted troth to him,
Till heart had fail'd and eye grown dim,—
       Waiting.

They said he never would come back,
Her only answer was, "Alack!
Then can this heart but find its rest
On one more faithful, and be blest,—
       Waiting."

At length the youth came back to find
Another suitor, one more kind,
To th' terrace swift he follow'd on,
Where maid and armèd knight stood lone—
       Waiting.

Nor turn'd she e'en one glance on him,—
Her eyes were fix'd, all glazed and dim,
On that strange knight who press'd her hand,
And whisper'd of another land,—
                    Waiting.

The thunder rumbled in the sky,
The sea-surge roar'd tumultuously,
Her mantle flutter'd in the wind,
Her hand within the knight's was shrined,—
                    Waiting.

The youth look'd on with evil eye,
Crept through the shadows stealthily,
At least he'd hear their whispers low,
At least her broken vows would know,—
                    Waiting.

He saw her head droop low, and lean
On the knight's breast;—fierce grew his mien,—
E'en heard her plead with him to bear
His bride to purer, holier air,—
                    Waiting.

Then stoop'd the knight, her slight form bore
With stalwart arm to the castle door,
Cross'd the dark draw-bridge with the fair,
Mounted his charger standing there,—
                    Waiting.

The charger champ'd his bit and paw'd,
And flung the foam-flecks on the sword
And corslet of the armèd knight,
Which glitter'd in the ghastly light,—
                    Waiting.

Then fleet as wind the courser flew
With wingèd feet, nor bridle knew,
Swift to the forest, out of sight,
Sped ladye-love and spectral knight,—
                    Waiting.

Now vanish'd hope, love's summer day,
To wint'ry frosts and shivering gray,
Loud swore the youth to avenge th' wrong,
With sword in deadly combat swung,—
                    Waiting.

Pale sun-rise broke the shadows gray,
On the cold flags the lover lay,
Like some enchanted sleeper kept
His vigil there, nor moan'd, nor wept—
      Waiting.

But lo! a foot-fall and a clang
Of sword and spear through silence rang,
He started to his feet—one blow—
He would the treacherous knight lay low
      For ever.

He drew his sword its blade to feel,
Then brandish'd high the glittering steel,
The knight drew his—his vizor raised,
Speechless the lover stood, and gazed
      For ever.

There stands he still, transfix'd in stone,
A statue, by rank weeds o'ergrown,—
Such is the legend told to me,
Of that weird statue by the sea,
      For ever.

Tho wild storms beat it night and day,
And ocean breakers toss their spray,
And eagles swoop and round it fly,
And lonely sea-gulls scream and cry
                    For ever.

Pitiless gusts athwart it sweep,
Remorseless rains upon it weep,
And salt waves dash their plumèd crests,
Then back retreat with mocking jests
                    For ever.

But still the statue stands unmoved,
As hearts should stand when love be proved.
This is tho legend's secret pure
Of faithful love that should endure
                    For ever.

And this tho legend old and weird,
Of that haunted castle lone and fear'd,
Where seven wither'd chestnut trees now loom
O'er that wild sea-strand's dreary gloom—
                    For ever.

THE SONG OF THE WIND.

IT croons within the chimney,
  In wild gusts shakes the pane,
And wails a low accompaniment
  To the fitful, rushing rain.

It whistles through the keyhole,
  On housetop lifts the slate,
And wrestles with the crazy blind,
  And grips the ill-swung gate.

Humming through the door-chink,
  Now rattling at the latch,
Moaning at the lattice-pane,
  Laughing through the thatch.

Is this all the wind has done
  To-night? O cruel wind!
Ask the madden'd ocean then,
  In mocking fury blind!

What says the surging deep,
    With wrecks and ruins strown?
The billows mock us as they drive—
    See what this wind has done!

Night of the loss of the " London," 1866.

" SHE'S GONE."

O young to die, so young—
    Life's day-dreams o'er,
Hast sewn the last stitch in her shroud,
    Or are there more?

So young to die, so young—
    Life's spells, joys o'er,
Has dimm'd the gold, has died the rose,
    Waiting for more?

So young to die, so young—
 Life's warfare o'er,
Has leaf'd the willow o'er her grave,
 Through winters hoar?

So young to die, so young—
 Life's friendships o'er,
Has bloom'd her amaranthine wreath
 On Heaven's own shore?

So young to die, so young—
 Death's victory o'er,
A white rose in her coffin lay,
 And grieve no more.

SEMPER EADEM.

THE moonlight waver'd in my dream,
　　It crept within my curtains' gloom ;
I said, Are all things as they seem
　　In this secluded moon-tryst room ?
　　　　　　O tell me !

I lured the moonlight, as it crept
　　From floor to ceiling as it sped,
I tried to court it ere I slept,
　　It laugh'd back on a golden head
　　　　　　Beside me.

It glanced too on the shadowy wall,
　　On a loved portrait, on a book,
But no where linger'd—dark grew all
　　Around me as the moon forsook,
　　　　　　Faint, trembling.

Aro all things as they seem? I said.
   On the gold hair pass'd that gold glow,
Then softly kiss'd the hands and head—
   Yes! one will be the same, I know,
            For ever.

The book may drop in dust away,
   The portrait fade, its colours die,
In vain the moon may smile some day,
   On these blank walls, when none are nigh—
           Earth's changes!

But love's light in the soul shall stay,
   And one thing will be e'er the same.
The head beside me turn'd—'twas day,
   The night was gone, the moon, my dream
           The same.

FOUND.

 WAS sitting one eve by the shore of the
    sea,
As lazy it rippled, retreated, and left
The print of its footsteps in sandals of foam,
With some weeds it had dropp'd, from sea-caverns
    reft.

There a jewel I found hid away by the wave,
A treasure once wreck'd from a casket long lost,
Where from groves of bright coral, few mysteries
    e'er
Come to breathe their lost secrets in whispers
    spray-tost.

I pick'd up the jewel all wet with the wave.
Thus trampled by ocean's swift sandals that roam.
On a gold thread I strung it, it hangs round my
    neck,
This gem from life's ocean, this star from its foam.

G

EXTREMES.

ROM the Madeleine came slowly
    A stately funeral hearse,
With its trappings and its velvet,
    And its plumes to nod averse,
As if pluck'd from Death's wings sable ;—
    I paused and held my breath,
For I saw it was a pageant
    From the solemn court of Death.

" Another from the court of Death,"
    So spake a passer-by,
And I but smiled a bitter smile,
    And do you ask me why ?—
" The court of Death," I answer'd him,
    The king then—where is he ?
Though true, the whole procession wore
    His royal livery.

The heavy pall of velvet black,
   Its fringe with silver deck'd,
The manes of ebon horses tied
   In plaits with silver fleck'd,
All pomp of woe, all grave-parade,
   This link of death to life,
This pride, alas! so pitiful,
   After life's ended strife.

Half buried 'midst this pomp of woe,
   Of ermine and of cloth,
Upon the coffin's shrouded lid,
   Death thus to woo not loth,
A wreath of winter roses lay,
   Exhaling frosty breath,
To make less insupportable
   This catafalque of Death.

Slowly the pageant moved along
   That crowded thoroughfare,
Now side by side with liveries,
   The rich, the gay, the fair,

A solemn moral pointing, as
    It wended slow along;
Like the solution of a discord
    In some impassion'd song.

But as I follow'd musingly
    The cortège on its way,
My ears were rudely startled by
    A coarse and vagrant lay,
Which from a ragged poor child came,
    Who sate at the palace gate,
And the burden of her distich sad
    I could not here repeat.

Hush, hush, poor child! I softly said,
    This is no place nor time
For ribald songs, for careless jests,
    With funeral bells to chime;
She raised a wondering face to mine,
    With look of mute surprise,
And the tears came quick, and clouded all
    The summer in her eyes.

Quaint were her childish answers, as
    My questions gently came,
She was born, she said, in misery,
    A very heir of shame ;
How young she was, thus drifting down
    The rapids of life's stream,
No hand of love to guard her feet
    Or sway life's treach'rous dream.

Upon the sparrows then I mused,
    The ravens too, that call
To th' ear that never closèd is,
    But open'd wide to all ;
And that Voice that once spake plainly
    On the shores of Galilee,
" Suffer the little children then
    To love and come to me."

Thus do extremes for ever meet
    On these highways of life,
Death leers sarcastic, as he points
    To Love with folly rife ;

To funeral honours paid by gold,
　　To coffins full of dust,
To living souls still cheated here
　　Of birthright and of trust.

Death's cortège still kept moving on,
　　Life's pageants giving place,
And heads were now uncover'd as
　　It enter'd *Père la Chaise;*
And up the sombre avenue,
　　To the grave's mysterious door,
Which, in mould'ring blackness gaping,
　　Waited one trophy more.

They lower'd down the coffin slow,
　　To oblivion and to dust,
Curtain'd in Death's pavilion drear,
　　With mildew, worm, and rust;
And now, too late for earth's regrets,
　　For tears in anguish shed,
Too late for mourners then to long
　　They'd been kinder to their dead.

Then home! And Fancy drew the sketch—
   The empty hearse, despoil'd
Of tenant, trappings, flowers, all—
   Its feathers wet and moil'd;
For cloud-tears that down kept dripping
   Beneath the veilèd sun,
Seem'd to mock this passing pageant
   For the dear and buried one.

Thick and fast the rain-drops fell
   On the living—on the dead,
But the child drew closer to me,
   To shelter her bare head;
Under an archway long we stood,
   More trustful grew the child,
And clung as if awaken'd from
   Some vision sad and wild.

O have we pass'd from death to life,
   From darkness into light,
From folly into wisdom's school,
   From faith to actual sight?

Such great extremes of life dismay,
    Bring questions to peruse,
Problems too intricate by far
    For me and my faint muse.

Death's sable terrors oft impose
    Dark mysteries on the mind,
While moral death of living souls
    We leave in thought behind;
We use life as a carnival,
    And wear a painted mask,
In self-approving consciousness,
    Till death for it must ask!

But carnivals must cease at length,
    And painted masks must fall,
And truth shall drive her chariot wheels,
    Triumphant, over all;
And falsehood, crime, oppression, sin,
    Shall reap the dues of dust,
When comes the judge to mark for aye
    The evil and the just.

How I yearn'd towards this orphan,
  Adrift upon the world,
Like a blossom from some lonely tree
  To swift destruction hurl'd,
Blown to some wretched corner lone,
  Neglected, starving, lost,
Trampled in dust by careless feet,
  Or nipp'd by death's swift frost.

Could I pluck this flower, I wonder'd then,
  Thrown vagrant on life's stream,
Defiled with vice and misery,
  Ere sunk in sin's mad dream?
For the petals of this wild weed were
  Still tender, young, and fair,
Although ragged were her garments,
  And matted was her hair.

Then I spoke of death, of Heaven,
  To this abandon'd child,
Of the goodness of our Father,
  Who on all who trust has smiled;

Of His patience and long-suffering
　　With the evil and the good,
Of our Master's deep compassion,
　　His death upon the rood!

Yea, the wondrous tale I told her,
　　Never tiring, ever new,
How Jesus, once a little child,
　　In Bethlehem's garden grew;
And all through His tender childhood
　　Was sinless and Divine,
And now in Heaven was waiting for
　　Her soul as well as mine.

Had I pluck'd, then, this poor wild weed
　　From pestilence of sin,
To lead her to the gates of pearl,
　　And cry—Lord, let her in?
Ere her garments were more mired and torn,
　　On paths perplex'd and base,
Could I teach, and hope to win her
　　To see her Father's face?

To listen to this story, as
  Slow pass'd that funeral car,
Oh yes! But since she's left me for
  A brighter world afar;
Death came, and loving took her, on
  One sweet, calm summer's night,
This flower I pluck'd from earth's dark paths,
  And fields of Sin and blight.

Not as the terror-king came he,
  No courtly pride he wore,
But as a peaceful messenger
  He enter'd at the door;
He took her, and he laid her down
  At the gates of endless day,
The face of Jesus to behold,
  The Refuge and the Way.

BARBARA.

THE night-wind raveth,
The rain-drop grieveth
Athwart the lattice—
Barbara, Barbara.

Within the old Tower,
Alas! for the bower
Where weepeth and watcheth
Barbara, Barbara.

Grim warriors look down,
And darkly they frown
From the gallery walls—
Barbara, Barbara.

The turret clock bell
Tolls its sad knell
On the wearying ear of
        Barbara, Barbara.

To the chapel she hieth,
Near her chamber it lieth,
Now passeth the corridor,
        Barbara, Barbara.

She kneels at the Altar,
Her fainting prayers falter,
She kneels not alone,
        Barbara, Barbara.

But one kneels beside her,
It is the black rider,
The false-hearted knight of
        Barbara, Barbara.

He sprang from the deep sea,
Swore ever to love thee,
For ever and ever,
        Barbara, Barbara.

He lifts the black casque,
Death hides in the mask,
He clasps to,his bosom
                    Barbara, Barbara.

That clasp stole the breath,
That kiss it was death,
Now frozen—a statue stands
                    Barbara, Barbara.

In the castell'd Erbrein,
That frowns on the Rhine,
Is this story in sculpture—
                    Barbara, Barbara.

The legend is old,
The story is told,
Alas for the lady !
                    Barbara, Barbara.

" THE LAST SUPPER."

LEONARDO DA VINCI.

AND still that silent Supper shines, shines
    on,
  From those dim walls, though convent walls
    no more,
As shone it on that brotherhood of monks,
  Many a wingèd century sung before,

When at their silent board they gazed as we,
  Upon those painted shadows on the wall,
The last mysterious Supper of the Twelve,
  Their pious love and reverence to recall.

It was a holy custom in those days,
  For Art to clasp commemorative each scene
Of Him who lowly lived, wept,—died for all,
  That we through pictures might feel what had
    been.

So when long ages in their solemn flight
  Should brush these records down with reckless
    wing,
And wipe their memories from the hearts of men,
  Their shadows still might live to comfort bring;

Of scenes all hallow'd by a Saviour's cross,
  And in Time's mazy halls for ever shine
From age to age the light of inspiration's touch,
  Which holy Art immortal shall enshrine.

So, they who on these trophies look to-day,
  And those, now dust, who've gazed before, ay,
    all!
E'en those to come who'll stand and gaze as we,
  Spell-bound, before a picture on a wall—

A crack'd and faded fresco, dim and old,
  Reflected shadows from a banish'd sun
Long since gone down with earlier Christian Art,
  Which modern schools must ever leave unwon.

Yet while we stand and gaze, we're minded of
    The " gray Gerolomite," the last of all
That brotherhood, whose touching words we
        quote,
    Which doth the " Spanish anecdote" recall—

How once a painter from a distant strand
    Did cross the wave, this picture great to see ;
The friar mark'd his wondering look, and thus
    Reply did make in speech austere but free—

" Stranger, thou gazest on a picture there,
    To me no picture e'en for many a year,
Though I am old, and my last sands near run,
    And soon these bones will rest upon the bier.

" When I review my youth, what I was then.
    What I am now, and ye beloved ones all,
I feel as if these were the living men,
    And *we* the colour'd shadows on the wall."*

Vide " Spanish Anecdote."

H

THE SONG OF THE REAPERS.

THEY sow to the wind, Lord, who sow not
      to Thee,
  For sowers and reapers we only are here,
Each hath his own acre in God's world to till,
  Ere the husbandman cometh his harvest to bear.

We each have our acre *alone* here to till,
    And must toil, if we hope some harvest to
      reap;
Be faithful and labour through sun and through
      rain,
    Ere night shall o'ertake us, and death's silent
      sleep.

If we sow to the wind, then the whirlwind we
      reap—
    " Do thistles bear figs, or grapes grow on the
      thorn ? "
If our wheat then we'd garner unsown by the tares,
  We must labour at noon-day, as well as at morn.

We have only our own prescribed acre to till,
    Not those of our neighbours, — only help them
        in need,
If the thunder-drops fall, or the heavy rains
        sweep,
    And their sheaves lie ungarner'd in paths where
        we tread.

'Tis then we must help them, and garner the
        sheaves,
    Safe housed from the tempest, or stored in the
        wain ;
While our plot will grow riper, nor lose e'en one
        sheaf,
    For a kindness love-render'd, not asking again.

They sow to the wind then who sow not to
        Him,
    The Lord of the harvest, who asketh no more
But that we pay back all our " talents" at last,
    And the sheaves we have bound, when He
        knocks at our door.

FAITH VERSUS PHILOSOPHY.

FIRST weave me a garment of fine thistle-
    down,
And a hat from the cobweb's sheer loom,
With a mantle fine spun from the gray mountain
    mist,
And then through the wide world I will roam
In search of Earth's reasons, God's truths to
    maintain,
And life's intricate problems thus prove,
Though 'twere better by far pride's ice-depths to
    break,
And accept what God hides in His love.

For can we perceive how the wild thistle grows,
    And the grass that we tread under foot,
Or how the fruit bursts from the blossom so
    sweet,
    Or the tree from its deep buried root ?

No, Nature's too coy her deep secrets to tell
   The most patient who sit at her feet;
We are shrouded in mystery without and within,
   And man's wisdom's a life-long defeat.

Philosophy proves but the sheer thistle-down,
   Swiftly trapp'd in a cobweb's fine snare,
Unbelief but a treacherous spider which waits
   To allure faithless souls to her lair.
Not required are we by our reason to prove
   Aught that Infinite Reason controls;
I know 'tis a wound to all self-love and pride,
   But beware of the infidel's shoals.

" We are bought with a price" by Him, who,
     forsooth,
   Makes conditions to level our pride,
We must sit in *Faith's* childhood, lie low at His feet,
   If we hope in His peace to abide—
All lowly and guileless by Calvary's cross,
   And apart from the world and its strife,
Is it hard to be children through earth's fleeting
     day,
   When if children, we're " heirs" of that life ?

Not the life that now is, with its sorrows and
    cares,
Contradictions, discrépancies, sin ;
But behind that great veil which o'er Calvary hung,
    When the Saviour for us enter'd in.

BUBBLES.

WE drift like bubbles down life's stream—
    Bubbles that sport with light,
Only reflect life's treacherous hues,
    Nor dream of sunless night.
When steals some breeze or flitting leaf,
    These bubbles break in air,
So exquisite they are, too frail
    A leaf-kiss e'en to bear.

With sails of silk we trim life's barque,
    With anchors silver-wrought,
Mann'd with bright hopes, our helmsman Self
    Gives sunken shoals no thought.

Alas ! we drift on Life's rough sea,
  Lash'd to a broken raft,
If Christ be not our pilot here,
  Heaven's breezes do not waft.

We hang our hopes on threads of gold,
  At least we think we do,
Spun from the loom of what we wish,
  Rather than what is true.
Alas ! these hang on cobwebs frail,
  Frailer than thistle-down,
Without our God cements the threads,
  And weaves them in a crown.

We tread Life's bridge of shadows, which
  Out of the mist is built,
Frail as the mirage in the sky
  That fades in sunset gilt.
Bubbles we are, on bubbles tread,
  Bubbles we court and grasp,
All, all so shadowy save that Love
  We might, but do not clasp.

If bubbles then, if shadows we,
   Who must in shadows grope,
There's comfort still in Christ's great Love,
   The Love which brings us hope.
No more like bubbles then we swim
   O'er waves of life's deep stream,
No more o'er shadows do we brood,
   Dark as life's saddest dream.

Shall we the lesson learn call'd Life,
   Ere yet this life is spun,
In shadows even find a key
   To pass Doubt's rubicon?
That light may then upon us flash,
   Life from our heart's-depths call,
Love's chrism rest upon our lips,
   His Love be all in all!

WAVE-FOOTSTEPS IN THE SANDS.

RIPPLING strings, soft touch'd
By breezes light,
Break ye in measures full,
Sing day and night.
Hark! the soft whisper—" hush!"
Steals o'er the strand,
And footprints of each wave
Indent the sand.

E'en steps of wandering waves,
That softly sweep,
Leave footprints in the sands
Where ripples creep.
While down the stately nave,
And transepts dim
Of ocean's wave-paved church,
We hear the hymn:—

" Thus leave your impress in
Earth's fleeting sand,
That others, following on,
May earnest stand
In the bright track you leave
On earth's pale shore,
When you have enter'd in
The golden door."

MEMORY'S BELLS.

OFTLY ringing, softly chiming,
Faintly tinkling, Memory's bells,
Chiming clear of vanish'd hours,
Golden hours, silvery peals,
When the hum of twilight trembles,
Ere soft clasp'd in dewy night,
When the flowers fold their petals,
Kiss'd to sleep by dying light.

When the night-breeze shakes the cypress,
  Moaning through each waving bough,
Chanting many a minor cadence—
  Æolian strings, that bode no woe!
When the Angelus, quick pealing,
  Calls the faithful ones to prayer,
Through the claustral shadows stealing,
  Alice, art thou with me *there?*

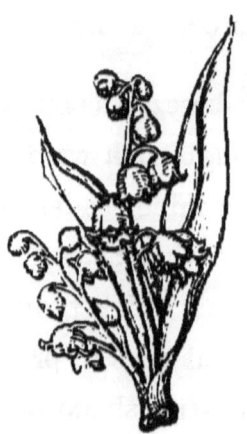

INTERVALS.

HANDEL.

THEN Handel's stately measured tread I
      heard
Marching adown Time's corridors revered ;
Immortal Handel, round whose score divine,
Enduring mysteries of Faith entwine
Their mazes.   Many seek to match thy power,
As torches mock the moon for some brief hour ;
Yea, scores of Imitators rise and swell
The ranks where thou, great master, lone shalt
      dwell ;
Thy genius leads where true art only reigns,
Binding the music-world in subtlest chains.
Awake ! great prophet of the solemn chords,
In song and chorus, make the inspired words !
While lesser lights shall flicker, waste, and die,
But leave to Handel Immortality !

SONNET.

WHEN Music wove in dreams her wizard
   spell,
From viol, harp-string, organ's flow and swell,
Unearthly concords lured my soul away
To lose herself in trance and ecstasy;
Beethoven pleaded, plaintive Weber sigh'd,
And Palestrina's solemn rhythm died,
Striking wild chords in memory's octaves deep,
Leaving me in my music-dream to weep;
Then wordless songs came floating on the hours,
Filling the air with gorgeous music-flowers—
Entranced within my dream, so rich and rare,
I lost the sense of sorrow, need, or care.
Alas! 'twas but a dream that so beguiled,
But I awoke again life-reconciled.

AN INVOCATION.

COME! nightly whisperer, come! though
    scarce divined,
Come, white-wing'd messenger, and gracious
    bring
Your words afloat upon the midnight wind;
In the night-watches hover round, and sing
Thoughts which e'en poets dare not call their
    own,
Yet fain would catch the echoes till the soul
Dares utterance in language rhythm-thrown.
Come then, bright spirit, in your light patrol,
Encamp and guard the threshold pure, serene—
Imagination's visionary sphere,
Whose star-lit chambers, hung with fancy's
    sheen,
Are peopled too. Be thou interpreter!
Chambers of imagery! may each threshold grow
Meet for an angel's feet to come and go!

THE SONG OF THE SEA.

AVE on then, rave on then, O desolate
  sea!
Rave on in your romance of dark mystery,
Fling up your spectral arms high from the deep,
Ay, fling them and toss them with passionate
  sweep.

And menace the rocks too that mock at your
  power,
As baffled, ye bound from the obstinate shore ;
And rave on, ay, rave on, O desolate sea !
Rave on in your wild world of strange mystery.

Nor tell but of those who have sunk to their rest
Deep down your green fathoms below the foam
  crest,
Nor of the bright gems in your dark coffers hid,
Iu grottos of coral that never shall fade ;

But tell me, ay, tell me, O desolate sea !
The burthen, the plaint, of your grand symphony ;
For not to lost treasures, or the dead that there
      sleep,
Is your burden sung ever in cadence thus deep.

For, at morn the waves sing it, O desolate sea !
And at night they repeat it, the same symphony,
For evermore chaunting the grand jubilee,
" Te Deum Laudamus," the song of the sea !

THE ANTHEM.

SWEEP the grand wave-chords full, O
     wind,
   With rippling fingers light,
Strike the rich keys which rise and fall
   To th' psalmody of night !

Ye glistening pebbles on the strand,
   Dragg'd backward by the sea,
Lend your clear treble, softly sweet,
   To this grand symphony.

Crash ! waves, upon the hoary rocks,
   And whirl your plumes of spray,
Flung from the chariot of the foam
   Death drives in 'reckless sway.

And ye, proud billows, rise to break
   Defiant in your might,
Swell the great anthem of the sea,
   The anthem of the night.

Come, Silence, on your dreamy wings,
   And fold them—let no flush
Of worldly care, or idle mirth
   Disturb this anthem—hush !

ADRIFT.

EAVE the helm, let go the oars,
   Fret no more the reckless wave,
Onward, seaward, let us float—
         Adrift !

Break the bubbles on the foam—
See the land in distance die ;
Onward, seaward let us float,—
Adrift !

Toss we on the boiling surge,
Passed the buoy, now out of sight—
Ocean, be thou antetype !
Adrift !

Passion on thy bosom sleep,
Laugh, pale sun-beams, o'er the waste ;
One word more, ay, one more clasp,—
Adrift !

Deep the soundings, yet how clear !
Mark the stones, the rocks, the weed—
You smile—dost read my meaning now,
Adrift ?

A WORD-PICTURE.

THE room was draped in shadows sombre,
      cool,
That trifled with the arras, as it flapp'd
Its heavy folds in idle Tuscan breeze,
That through the lattice pane came wandering in.
Here a great painter at his easel sat,
Limning the tender features of a face
That shyly look'd from out a modest veil,
Like some sweet exile from yon clouded sphere,
Or distant planet gazing down on us
Poor mortals, who in dreams can only find
(Not always *then*) such faces peerless quite,
As sculptured from an alabaster rock,
Yet sensitive and varying as the harp
Æolian, trembling to the summer breeze;
And eyes—O wondrous eyes! like looking down
Those soundless depths of Leman's quivering
      blue,

Which lure in vain the soul to sound those deeps;
The hair, too,—where the sunset laid her palm,
Has tangled in its tresses skeins of gold.
Now dream the minstrels o'er their golden chords,
Stirring the air to hush of music's thralls;
The rebeck and the lute breathe music-words,
As fast the painter weaves his colours in,
Essays his best to counterfeit that face
Upon the canvas wakening to his touch.
The lady's eyes are never fix'd on him,
Her head is half-averted, turn'd to mark
A figure standing by the painter's side,
With finger raised, as if he said,—Take care,
With reverence touch the shadows even mine.
She sits, the lady, on the dais raised—
From the oak screen, with cornice richly carved,
Hangs soft folds of drapery round her head,
Like a mosaic background wrought in air
By checker'd rays of sunlight's prisms bright,
Her hound in glossy coat lies at her feet,
And upward gazes at his mistress' face.
'Tis Laura, Petrarch's Laura, as she sits,
'Tis Petrarch by the painter's chair who stands,
'Tis Simon Memmi, he alone who dares

Upon that shred, that perishable shred
Of canvas there to lay creative tints,
And bid them counterfeit fair Laura's face—
This is the picture, sweet, commemorate,
Of Petrarch's Laura and of Petrarch's love.

A NEW GONDOLA SONG FOR VENICE, IN 1866.

UT the Queen has come back,
   The Queen of the Sea,
No longer an exile
   Nor widow is she.

They stole her regalia,
   They trampled her power,
Usurp'd her dominion,
   And pilfer'd her dower.

They emptied her coffers,
   They mock'd at her pride,
Wore even the jewels
   Of Italy's bride !

But the Queen has come back,
   The Queen of the Sea,
Her crown is redeem'd, and
   Our Venice is free !

No more the oppressor
   Shall plant his proud heel
On th' grave of San Marco,
   Or bid Venice kneel.

No—the Queen has come back,
   Unfetter'd and free,
She has dropt all her weeds
   In th' grave of her sea.

Her gems and her pictures
   Are now all her own,
And the fair Queen, Venetia,
   Sits high on her throne.

THE "NIGHT AND MORNING," OF
MICHAEL ANGELO.

GREAT Angelo! His sinewy arm has
     hew'd
From living rock the block from which he strikes
The sparks from hammer wielded in his might;
And then the finer work begins, and now
The chisel in its office keen and sharp,
Cuts, shapes, proportions in th' incongruous mass—
The file the task completes with cunning skill,
And lo! the statues " Night and Morning" live!
O in that chapel where the shadows steal,
To hang their draperies o'er sepulchral urns,
There pause they, reverently kneel and fold
Their hands before this grand unfinish'd thought,
Veiling the silent faces, till we dream
Of beauty ideal as that Poet dream'd,
Who left this work for shadows to complete
With their weird fingers, pencilling each face,
Till e'en far grander is this rough-hewn thought,
Than if express'd, and that great dream dream'd out.

THE CALL.

THE fountain drips echoless her low minor
    phrase,
And the willow droops wooingly down through
    the maze,
She droops till she half blends her life with the
    stream
Whose bubbles she breaks, like the thread of a
    dream.

And the nightingale calls from the darks of the
    pine,
To her mate to come back to his own leafy shrine,
Then she waits for the answer, borne back on the
    breeze,
Low whisper'd by flowers, and repeated by trees.

O list to the pining chord, ever and oft,
Hark! hark! comes the cadence so plaintive and
    soft,

" Take the thorn from my breast," this all sadly
    she sings,
" Then hide me, safe hide me, love, under thy
    wings."

The red shield of Mars seems to guard the sweet
    grove,
In the silence of night and the silence of love,
All is dark save the glimmer of Autumn's red
    star,
With the link of two hearts that united now are.

A PORTRAIT.

AROUND her neck Love's corals hang,
    Truth's pearl shines in her heart,
An aureole halo girts her head
    With Wisdom's better part.

About her wrists Strength's sapphires cling,
  Her hands with rubies flame,
Faith's wingèd sandals bind her feet—
  Now, canst thou guess her name?

The law of Kindness gilds her tongue—
  Forbearing to the weak,
She patiently forgives the wrong,
  In wrath is slow to speak.

Forgetting self in others' weal,
  In Love and Truth complete,
Meekly she bears her cross through life,
  And waits at Jesu's feet.

FLOWERS FOR PARADISE.

HAT plants are these? what flowers sweet
    and rare,
That skirt earth's paths of sorrow, sin, and care,
That meekly hide 'mid shadows cool and shy?
Save for their fragrance we should pass them by,
Yet careless footsteps often on them tread,
Though bend they not, nor break, nor e'en are
    dead,
But from each bruisèd stalk faint perfume flies,
Of resignation to the bending skies.
Life's forest, with her endless, devious ways,
Her pathless copses lead to 'wildering maze,
Her dizzy heights, abysses black and deep,
To crags, dark ravines, and to chasms steep;
Her evanescent rainbows, where the sun
Out of a cloud a fleeting dream has spun,
Gorgeous as fleeting, beautiful as bright,
Yet while we gaze quick swooning on the sight;
But these fair flowers not everywhere are seen,

In paths of earth, so pure in shape and mien.
But such the souls—the meek, the chaste, the
  true,
Life-flowers that light the path our steps pursue
On earth, celestial plants for ever fair,
Which scent life's wastes, perfume earth's desert
  air,
And God is watching, waiting in His skies
For them to bloom with Him in Paradise !

A SONG FOR THE CRITICS.

ES, indeed we must sing, dear Critics,
  although
You over our cages a handkerchief throw,
If one streak of pale sunshine should steal through
  a chink,
I'm afraid we shall chirp still, whatever you
  think !

But the best way to manage us seems, after all,
Not to clip our wings utterly, lest we should fall—
Put a lump of white sugar, at times, in the cage,
We shall sing all the sweeter, or try, we'll
　　engage,
Till at length we half win you to say we aspire.
We are not all nightingales,—would that we
　　were !—
There are larks, and to sing e'en the chaffinches
　　dare,
For all have a voice in Dame Nature's bowers,
And all have their part in life's passing hours;
For not only the lark pours rhythms of sound,
But we're told not a sparrow falls aye to the
　　ground
Without the sure knowledge of Him who hath
　　made
The bird for the sunshine, the bird for the shade.
So be patient, dear Critic, with all that must sing,
If their notes are not false, no mocking-bird's
　　wing;
We are not like the rest of the world, as you
　　know,
We are fanciful, sensitive—breezes may blow

Our song-notes away, so have patience with all,
And if you can't praise us, O what will befall ?
Shall we chirp, warble still, in the shades of life's
    bowers,
If not in the noontide, through twilight's sad
    hours ?
Some pilgrim may hear us in travel-stained
    dust,
And lay down his staff, and sandals adjust,
Refresh'd by some carol, go forth on his way,
And bless some small wood-bird who sang such
    a day.

THE DANCE.

A BALLAD.

ONLY another dance, he urged—
    The king's son, it was he,
And Beatrix stood in her shining robes,
    As the lady of minstrelsy.

K

Only another dance—he cried,
 Sounding the depths of her eyes—
To the wars I go ere to-morrow's sun
 Over the East shall arise.

But Beatrix raised those wonderful eyes,
 Half doubtful, then she sprang—
As if throwing away some memory
 Of a song she once had sung—

So into that dance she flings herself,
 So giddy, reckless seems,
While her peerless face and her wondrous eyes,
 Woo gazers to fond love-dreams.

Half-awed, the king's son led her on,
 As if 'twere profanity
To lead such a lady to a dance
 In a night of revelry.

Though reverent he clasp'd the proffer'd hand,
 As she dropt it in his own—
'Twas clasp'd in the warrior's bronzèd palm,
 As a pearl in some dark shell thrown.

THE DANCE.

The music dream'd, the dance began,
  Her hand the warrior press'd—
How beat her heart 'neath clouds of lace,
  Upon that warrior's breast !

A rose fell from the wreath she wore,
  Encircling the wavy gold,
He caught it—but little she reck'd or knew
  Of this his theft so bold.

A strange repose stole o'er her soul,
  Unlike the fever-gleam
Which once had blazed within her heart,
  But proved a waking dream.

She could have died that hour in peace,
  He could have died with her—
O what a dance for life was that
  Which hearts to their depths could stir !

At length she breathed her answer to
  His deep, impassion'd sigh,
Too long she had listen'd for her peace
  On that night of revelry.

Slow came her words: " I may not wed,
  Betrothed I long have been,
Though he is false,, and a faithless knight,
  I keep my heart's vows clean.

" Nor can this promise be forgot,
  It was heard in holy heaven;
I must be true, though he be not,
  For my troth before God was given."

Then the king's son bent down on her
  A look of speechless love;
Was this a partner for a dance,
  Or an angel from above?

He mused, he sigh'd, and then he knelt
  As praying at a shrine,—
" Beatrix, guardian of my soul,
  O one day thou'lt be mine!"

She heard, she wept, and whisper'd—" Go,
  Till some sweet summer's day,
When June shall bring her roses back,
  And break all thralls away."

It was a death to either heart,
  No troth could then be given,
No cup of love might either taste,
  Since old chains were not riven.

To war he went, the king's own son,
  With one rose on his breast—
One faded, wither'd ball-room rose,
  Close to his heart was press'd ;

Caught from the fluttering lace that veil'd
  A fluttering heart beneath,
And I trow the warrior who caught it then,
  Will wear it through life and death.

THE SEQUEL.

O bring me my lute—it hangs on the yew,
　　In the bower by the clematis spread;
Then cut me some roses all dripping with dew,
　　Half open—the white and the red.

Thus Beatrix spoke, that sweet desolate maid,
　　As out to the terrace she stole,
Where the moon ghastly smiled over bower and
　　　　glade,
　　And the nightingale warbled her dole.

Now bring me my casket, e'en here where the
　　　　moon
　　May look on my treasures and gems,
For under night's spell I would count them o'er
　　　　soon,
　　While they rival the stars' diadems.

Thus Beatrix stole to her bower all hid
  In clematis, myrtle and rose,
And with a deep sigh she uplifted the lid,
  And mused long in silent repose.

Then out of its cell a small locket she drew,
  'Twas a heart with red rubies a-glow,
And a name there was set in the deep sapphires
    blue,
  Like a flame lit on drifts of the snow.

Then trembled her hand, and though light was
    the press
  On the fine subtle magical spring,
It brought out the gold of a marvellous tress,
  And one black as the raven's own wing.

Down, down in the leaves this locket she press'd,
  Deep down in a dark silent grave ;
Thus she buried the love which once glow'd in
    her breast,
  With the gift that her false lover gave.

Then back to the castle sweet Beatrix steals,
   When the moon has forsaken her bower,
With her lute, and her casket, but nought that
     reveals
   The tale of that strange midnight hour.

But the rose that the king's son wore on his breast,
   And the king's son, whither is he?
For the false knight sleeps with a lance in his
     breast—
   And Beatrix's soul now is free.

AN UNANNOUNCED VISITOR AT
THE TUILERIES.

SAW ye not the shadow
    That pass'd through the palace gate,
Up the broad steps, and through the door,
   And enter'd the halls of state?

AT THE TUILERIES.

Passing each wary sentinel,
    Not as a stranger might,
Who for the first time feels her way
    Where new scenes meet her sight;

But as one long familiar
    With those galleries and halls,
The crystal lamps, the gilded bronze,
    And frescoes on the walls.

On, on the shadow glided swift,
    Enter'd the Hall of Peace;
Before an equestrian statue paused,
    And whisper'd "Blest release."

The statue of an exiled king,
    From throne and country driven,
'Twas broken, defaced, this effigy
    To ruin's empire given.

A deep sigh from the shadow came,
    That gazed upon the king,
A sigh that rent th' historic air,
    As memories round it cling.

Then onward, slow, the shadow moved,
  Enter'd the banquet hall;
Glory and splendour fill'd that space,
  With music's syren thrall.

Imperial splendour dazed the eye,
  And pomp and pageant shone;
Yet jewell'd cups and ruby wine
  Hid not the " skeleton."

For close to the imperial chair
  The shadow stole, and leant
Upon the velvet and the gold,
  With eye and ear intent.

They spoke of one now queen no more,
  But exiled, banish'd, dead,
Who in these regal halls had once
  Mild radiance on them shed.

Some said, " A pity dire it was
  That once a random shot
Had not released one martyr's woes,
  And saved one weary lot."

And others spoke, but none could urge
    One harsh word of the dead ;
But all concurr'd that virtues rare
    Were on this princess shed.

That true as mother, chaste as wife,
    By sorrow bent, not broken,
Meekly she bore her cross on earth,
    And left her griefs unspoken.

Calm in her dignity had braved
    The exile's lonely part
In the adopted home she found,
    In England's noble heart.

At this the shadow slowly moved
    Toward the draperied door,
Pausing an instant as it pass'd
    Before the Emperor.

Then came a voice upon the air,
    Not weird, not harsh, not dreary,
But soft and low as river's flow,
    On summer nights so eerie—

" Earthly crowns to dust must turn,
    Sceptres to broken reeds ;
Kingdoms will shake, thrones be usurped,
    And queens wear widows'-weeds."

Then came a cold blast through the hall,
    Lights to their sconces quiver'd ;
Beauty and flattery dropp'd their masks,
    And Pleasure's phantoms shiver'd.

Then down the glittering stairs she stole,
    Guards, muskets, all unheeding,
Close by the sentries on she went,
    No earthly summons heeding.

" Je suis mieux," * the last words fell
    Slow on the midnight air,
And the ghost that haunted the Tuileries,
    Vanish'd through mist and glare.

* Last words of Queen Amalie.

CHRISTMAS ROSES.

A BUBBLE of glass, frail Venice glass,
    These Christmas roses to hold—
So graceful the pedestal of my vase
    Tight clasp'd in these claws of gold.

While here and there sparkles a ruby red,
    And Orient jewel bright,
To mirror my roses and softly shed
    A holy celestial light.

Roses in winter! thus sweet and rare,
    This Christmas morning shall bring
The thought of one Rose more radiant far,
    Dropt to-day from the crown of the king.

FOOTSTEPS LEFT 'IN AN EGYPTIAN
TOMB THREE THOUSAND
YEARS.

THE dead, the dead, the winged centuries
        sing !
O'er Lybia's golden sands they fold the wing,
Brooding o'er those colossal urns which hide
Ashes of Egypt's kings, of Egypt's pride.

Here sleep they on, nor grim corruption know,
Embalm'd in state, in mocking gear of woe,
Cheating the silent banquet of the worm,
With gold and gems which deck each mummied
      form.

Still sleep they on, nor Time their pride can steal,
Each in his rock-hewn chamber, where the seal
Ruthlessly broken from the sculptured door,
Yawns, but in vain Oblivion to implore ;

Where wild beasts range, and vultures see their
    prey,
Where jackals cry, bats wheel, and spectres stray,
Hiding 'mid sculptures on the storied walls,
'Mid baffling scrolls which science e'en appals.

The wingèd globe surmounts each sacred door,
Type of eternity for evermore;
How perfect every symbol, no decay
Is here, but sharp as chisell'd yesterday.

Mocking our wonder with strange types and
    wings,
Which guard these death-homes of Egyptian
    kings,
Where still the shifting sands drift high and deep,
Around the doors where golden Ages weep.

So cool, so dry, these chambers of the dead,
So spicy, these death's cerements, where we tread—
O wither'd mummies mocking monarchs' state,
Walk'd ye once Karnac's halls now desolate?

Are we the first, too, that have enter'd here,
For thousand, thousand years look'd on this bier ?
Shade of Osiris ! dost thou haunt the gloom,
As we profane with steps thy kingly room ?

No, not the first of bold intruders here
Since these lost footsteps left the lonely bier,
The frozen silence thaw'd, and all reveal'd
When Mariette the charmèd door unseal'd ;

To mark strange footsteps Ages trod before,
The sand so clear indented from the door,
Up to the very couch where Apis lay,
Footprints as fresh as printed yesterday.

O frozen silence ! stillness marvellous,
That held these mortal imprints e'en to us,
What spell of Ages broke when light reveal'd
This wondrous record which those Ages seal'd !

Footprints to write a story in a verse,
Where science baffled, feebly can rehearse
These sculptured records of long Ages dead,
Lost and forgotten, to oblivion wed.

Too soon the wind came though, with reckless
    breath,
And bird and beast, to track the path of death,
Erasing these memorials in a tomb,
And those last footsteps that awoke the gloom.

Thus History writes upon this sandy floor,
A verse more plaintive than a requiem's score,
Treading in footsteps left three thousand years—
Echoes! bring back your lachrymal for tears!

Ay, wake yon echoes from your dreamless sleep!
From shadowy recesses light-ward creep,
We call—alas! ye answer in a tongue
Unknown to us, long lost the dead among.

O land of Egypt, mystery and dreams!
By prophets sung—for reverie what themes!
O fallen columns, broken architraves,
Æolian wailing o'er thy desert raves!

Raves for a land o'ershadow'd still by wings,
Dark land benighted though a land of kings;
The dead, the dead, sing, wingèd centuries! sing
O funeral harp, with mute and shatter'd string!

L

But tell us, tell us of these footsteps here—
Whose were they last to leave this sepulchre ?
Echoes, wild echoes ! with the shadows weep,
For golden Ages here for ever sleep.

None may awake them from the dreamless dead,
Save wand'ring spirits, who with phantom tread
Leave us no footprints of their noiseless feet,
But come and go, and solemn vigils keep.

Wing on then, cycles ! golden cycles, wing !
In Egypt's twilight, her lost centuries sing,
Sing of the dead, forgotten, shrouded land,
Which mocks us but with footsteps left in sand.

THE ARNO AT NIGHT.

BRIGHT bubbles of glass imprison the
       flames
  Which lighten the bridge swung over the stream,
Down dropping reflections in the swift flood,
    Like organ pipes shatter'd in silvery gleam.

The ripples, too, vibrate in cadences soft,
    To the spirit of night which fingers the keys
That form in the current that eddies along,
    Breathing its lay to the wandering breeze.

It is only a river, methinks ye may say,—
    A long row of lamps swung over a stream;
A stretch of mere fancy, the organ pipes too,
    And as to the music, an enthusiast's dream !

You smile—but the Poet finds " sermons in stones,"
    Ay, " Books in the brooks," even music at call ;
" Poor Poets" ye call us, but we can smile too,
    And sing although no one may listen at all.

TO ————.

DO you understand me, Jessie,
    How I mean to wear your ring ;
Only one condition making,
    Which a smile or tear may bring ?

If to wear your ring " for ever,"
    One short promise I must have—
If I change my mind to-morrow,
    You'll take back the ring you gave.

Such a long word is " for ever,"
    And if this hand should drop to dust,
Whose will then the ring be, Jessie ?
    I think I'll wait before I trust.

Too many rings echo " for ever,"
    And too many " thine alone ;"
Too many hearts are link'd to gold-dust,
    Some grow chisell'd into stone !

We're all too prone to say " for ever,"
    E'en a wedding ring may rust ;
I think I'll wait, Dear, till to-morrow—
    Can *you* wait, and will you trust ?

THE DESERTED CHÂTEAU,

MIROMENIL, ARQUES.

GIRT by a stately park, the Château stands
    In sombre grandeur, desolate and
        drear,
Only the rooks are left as tenants now,
    To haunt the shadows in the beeches near ;

Within the tower's gloom, the sparrows build,
    And weeds grow rank on door and window
        sill,
While flap the shutters on the broken glass,
    Which once the stainèd oriel did fill ;

The weather-beaten clock is silent, dumb,
  No more it answers to the flight of hours ;
The bell is only swung by wayward winds,
  And life exists alone in passing flowers.

The cunning spider weaves her subtle loom
  Around the spacious windows, where no
    face
Has look'd to answering face for many a year,
  In haunted halls and gloom-spun dreary
    space ;

The ivy drapes the tottering garden wall,
  The beech-tree drops her thin dejected boughs
Untrimm'd, and snapp'd away from rusty nails,
  While sickly fruit just dropp'd, the border
    strews ;

The garden roller stands just where 'twas left
  When last the gravel walk it careful roll'd,
All wash'd and worn by blanching rains in bed
  Of towering weeds, half buried in the mould ;

One straggling vine the glassless hot-house fills,
  The mildew'd grapes drop sullen from their
    stalks ;
Which no hand gathers—left to rot and rains,
  Or peck'd in secret night by vagrant hawks ;

And on the lawn the grass grows wild and
    rank,
  The briar has usurped the gay parterres,
The gaunt arms of the cedars, threaten weird
  In mocking pride among the statelier firs ;

The weeds have trampled out the gravell'd walks,
  No traces scarcely of the paths remain ;
We muse o'er rustling trains, and rich brocades,
  And silvery laughter never heard again ;

The moat is dry, and choked with briar and
    brake,
  And wild weeds trample insubordinate,
And Desolation rampant stalks uncheck'd,
  From park to lawn, from Château door to gate.

Ah ! what tradition haunts the ghostly place ?
 What glamour rests upon the silent scene ?
What wizard's spell with evil mesh has wove
 This veil of mystery over what has been ?

The echoes only mock us when we ask,
 And wild rooks as they caw from leafy towers,
And shadows ring the changes on the key
 Of the same score that's writ by gorgeous
  flowers.

They breathe it ever to the rising sun,
 And when they glorify God's bright noon-day,
They sigh it when the coffin lid shuts down—
 The mournful Coronach—all has past away !

153

A LEGEND.

E knew he could not tempt her, though a
       throne
He had to offer, and a crown of gold
With priceless jewels on her brow to blaze;
He knew he could not win her, though unwon,
Unpledged she was, and even free to love—
Yet might she not aweary grow some day,
Weary of sitting on that doorstep lone,
Plying her distaff from the golden dawn,
Until the bats brought night upon their wings?
And would she never spin that long thread out,
And then look up towards that beetling cliff,
Where stood the castle in its towering strength?
Yet reck'd she not that castle on the hill,
Nor its proud inmate in his lonely gloom.
Flower of the hamlet was fair Geraldine,
And to the Virgin vow'd from cradle life,
But now an orphan was she in that Grange;

Only her old nurse fill'd her mother's place—
For she in churchyard peace long, long had slept.
And yet the baron still gazed down in hope
From battlemented walls on that lone house,
Where—save the great mill, long since wreck'd,
        disused,
Which spread its arms, as if in threatening mood,
Over the reckless stream that long since had
All barrier burst, soft rippling on its way
O'er mossy stones and ferns, and flag-leaves
        broad—
No other object in that valley lone,
Hinder'd the baron's view of that doorstep
Where sat fair Geraldine with distaff e'er,
Plying the thread that never seem'd to end.
Still young the baron was, an orphan too,
And comely, thus the village maidens said ;
And when, in earlier days, these two did meet,
And play together by that mill-stream's flow,
Stringing wild cowslips on the same silk thread,
Then would he whisper—" Geraldine, some day
My little wife wilt be, and thou shalt wear
Brocade of gold, and drop these home-spun robes ;
Instead of cowslips round thy golden hair

A coronet of precious gems shalt wear."
And she his Queen should be, his Queen of May,
And they should wedded be in Mary's month.
But then her mother died, her first great grief,
She had no room within her heart for else
Than tears and lamentations ; and the youth
Was sent from home in foreign wars to fight ;
And after many a year, at last came back,
And brought his bride, who only lived a year,
And with her babe slept in that churchyard too.
Then wistful gazed the baron toward the Grange,
And, tempting, offer'd her his hand once more,
For memory had upturn'd those early flowers
Of other days, when they were children both.
But no—she would not wed him now, she said,
For a sweet lady, clad in holy white,
With a fair child she held, came there one night,
(And gossips said a vision she had seen
Of Blessed Mary and the Holy Child)
And she had whisper'd to fair Geraldine
To wed her soul to heaven, not to earth,
And bid her knot some golden threads she
        brought,
And spin a veil, and then a robe to make

With this same thread—thus work'd she night
    and day,
From golden dawn until the bats brought night;
And when the veil was spun, and robe was made,
She back would come. Thus Geraldine did spin,
Nor wept she o'er the quiv'ring woof she held;
But one day, when the baron came to see
If she her task had done, he found her—but
Standing within a golden sheen of light,
Array'd in bridal robe and virgin veil,
Waiting, she said, until that lady came
With the crown'd child within her tender arms;—
She came,—and led her through the churchyard's
    rest,
Into the golden cloisters of her home.
He watch'd them from the doorstep disappear
Down through the churchyard into shadows merge,
But on the doorstep where she'd sat so long,
Her distaff lay and its last spinning spun;
Up from the step he raised it to his lips,
And press'd a holy kiss upon the thread,
The golden thread that Geraldine had left
To draw his soul to hers and Paradise.

THE LIGHTHOUSE OF AILLY,

NORMANDY.

HERE stands a lighthouse on that cliff
　　Which overhangs the sea,
And brightly shines through rain and mist,
　　The star of lone Ailly.

A lantern-star, the ships to warn
　　From that all dangerous cliff,
Where centuries long the sea has waged
　　With rocks and reefs, her strife.

For miles far outward, o'er the main
　　Is seen this star's bright blaze,
This ocean-star, which never wanes,
　　Nor dims in deepest maze.

Alas! this lighthouse on the cliff
　　Is doom'd,—for on that ledge
On which it stands, the sea below
　　Is grappling with each wedge—

Each rocky wedge that holds that cliff,
 And guards that lighthouse there
Where looms the lantern of the sea,
 And guides the mariner.

What mad device that rear'd this tower
 Upon this crumbling ledge,
Where Nature's barrier is worn away
 By Ocean's hostile siege?

Already has been swept away
 By the remorseless sea,
One half that cliff and more, where stands
 The light of lone Ailly.

And thus that beacon on the cliff
 That overhangs the sea,
Is doom'd to fall, to wane some day—
 The star of lone Ailly.

THE LEGEND OF THE CHURCH OF VARENGEVILLE, NORMANDY.

A LITTLE farther on that cliff—
On that same treacherous verge,—
There stands the Church of Varengeville,
Where beats the same wild surge;

Of which Tradition thus relates
A legend quaint and old,
To drape the Church of Varengeville
With interest untold.

Saint Valery—thus the legend runs—
Was an apostle here,
And Abbé of Leuconaüs, once
The wildest district near.

The villagers had brought the stones
To build their church, within
The hamlet,—in a field hard by,—
All ready to begin.

But one dark night, the holy saint
    Removed the stones to where
The church was built, to crown a crag
    On this wild cliff so bare.

Between the earth and heaven it rests,
    E'en like a floating barque,
For winds and waves to homage bring,
    And this lone church to mark.

'Twould seem as if no hand of man
    Had been so daring—placed
This shrine upon a crumbling rock,
    To tempt the wave and blast.

A hundred times by lightning struck,
    By tempests torn and riven,
Its roof, and tower, and windows wreck'd,
    Yet still it points to heaven.

Alone upon that sombre cliff
    Where boils the surge below,
Its seething depths like lava floods,
    Threatening its overthrow;

Yet still the church of Varengeville
   Burns bright her beacon light,
Her vestal flame lights Mary's shrine,
   Undying day and night.

And through the stainèd window gleams
   This beacon night and day,
'Twould seem the saint did feed the flame
   To light that stormy bay,

And that the legend might be true—
   For she has braved all ill,
Ocean and tempest, war and strife,
   Sweet church of Varengeville.

Nor doomèd is her light to wane,
   Star of the sea ! bright star !
From Mary's shrine send forth your rays,
   And light earth's wanderer !

ALPINE ECHOES.

ECHO.

 DEFT magician of the silent wood,
  O moon-loved wizard of the sleeping
   lake,
The rivers, streamlets, answer to thy mood,
  And turn to music for an echo's sake!
Thou witching minstrel of the hill and glade,
  Thou saucy mimic by the bubbling rills,
Now coy, now bold, shy phantom of the shade,
  The glamour of thy voice the senses thrills,
  Echo, fond playmate of the nightingales!

Mocking the eagle in her eerie high,
  At hide and seek behind the Alpine cliff;
Ringing the changes on the bittern's cry,
  Awak'ning silence in rock-realms where life

Stands like a skeleton, whose wither'd bones
   Grimly rehearse of death, and spirit fled !
To most of us earth's solitudes breathe tones
   Which only wail the dirges of the dead,
   Though Nature ought the soul to life-schools
     lead.

When veiled the hours are in their mantle gray;
   When climbs the moon above the high Alps,
     like
A lily broken from her stem away,
   Dropp'd on a bank of greenish cloud—like streak
From some parterre detach'd from gardens where
   No foot of earth e'er trod the silver wheat;
Nor full this lily moon, though peerless, fair,
   Fairer than when it blooms with jewels set,
   To deck Night's swarthy brow with coronet;—

Then calls the nightingale, from bowers among
   Dark dewy shrines, his exiled mate in woe
Now pleads, now cries, now pours his plaintive
     song
   In lavish fulness, whistling soft and low ;

Then Echo, laughing, from her couch upsprings,
    And flings the cadence back in witching trills,
And the shy bird in flutt'ring haste swift wings,
    Till Silence, like a prayer, the silence fills,
    And Night's Æolian harp the darkness thrills !

O mountain, rill, and crag, and whispering grove,
    How mute your tongues and lock'd your parchèd
        lips !
O myrtle-bowers, grottos laurel-wove,
    How lifeless, dumb, save for fond Echo's steps,
The witching prattler of Eve's dusky court,
    Whose spells weave round us many a subtle
        thread !
Coy phantom, in thy mocking triumphs short,
    Echo, immortal minstrel, thou wert made
    To haunt this Alp-land wilderness and glade !

AN ALPINE EXCURSION.

MY eyes were shut, I was dreaming
    Of our walk, Dear, yesterday,
When a crowd of pictures, thronging,
    Filled memory's cloisters gray.

How high was that crag down-shelving
    To that forest sombre and dim!
How steep was that path untrodden
    To solitudes known but to Him!

How hush'd was the sound of our voices,
    While listening to streamlet and leaf,
And filling our hands with the flowers
    Of Alpine's summer so brief!

How long, Dear, we sat there dreaming,
  Entranced by the air and scene,
Under that rock in the shadow,
  That rock of foreboding mien.

The flowers all blooming around us,
  And fringing the whispering rills,
Orchis, gentiana, primula,
  Rhododendrons, and bright daffodils.

And in damp, odorous fissures
  Where waved the rich plumelets of fern,
And trembled in light dewy freshness
  The maiden-hair too in her turn.

Then upward and onward toiling,
  We reach'd the crags of fresh snow,
Close to the cataract's thunder,
  Which leap'd to the valley below,

Tearing great roots of the pine-tree,
  And hurling them down in its tide,
Leaping in fury and madness,
  So mighty in joyance and pride.

Far up that perilous mountain,
   A lonely small châlet we reach'd,
The flowers still clung to the threshold,
   Though Alp-storms the brown walls had bleach'd;

No smoke now curl'd from the chimney,
   And no footsteps trampled the weeds,
Or the long grass worn to a footpath,
   Or scatter'd the waving grass-seeds.

Yet there in its picturesque loneness,
   Away from all stir and all life,
Stood this frail little storm-beaten châlet,
   So far from the world and its strife.

How long we sat there by that streamlet
   That had broken away from its course
In a deep trough, rough-hewn from the pine-log,
   So instinct with wild freedom's force !

It trickled, it dripp'd on the green sward,
   It illumined the flowers' brief dream,
I drank of that fresh mountain rillet,
   And bathed my hot brow with the stream.

Then lo, through the arch of the forest
    Came arrows to herald the moon
Which lit up this forest cathedral
    From shadows, to mimic the noon.

Then came low chanting of voices,—
    The nightingale he heard it too,
First he call'd, then he trill'd, then he warbled,
    His wandering love-mate to woo.

And the insects around us, they heard it,
    And in their fine treble join'd in
With the deep rolling bass of the torrent,
    And the leaves rustling—zephyrs to win.

The châlet turn'd all to bright silver,
    The windows of crystal look'd out,
No longer recall'd the rough cedar,
    Once toss'd by the storm-winds about.

The crags into amethyst changing,
    The green to rock emerald's light,
The flowers—O loves of the angels !
    Do ye drop them unseen here at night ?

Did they fall from your gold crowns yonder,
  As earthward, on missions of love,
Ye sowed them to light our steep pathway,
  Till we reach your bright gardens above ?

Thus with eyes shut I have been dreaming
  Of our walk, Dear, of yesterday,
And here are the pictures I've brought you
  From memory's cloisters away.

" EVEN THERE ALSO."

N cathedral aisles of a forest dim,
    Where the shadows creep to pray,
And the sunlight thrills through the traceried
    roof
Of the pine trees' stately sway ;

On a knoll we sat with the pine-cones spread,
  Sweet odours from bowers of spruce
Wafted their fragrance around us like
  Sweet fancies that dreams unloose.

The realm of glacier above us slept,
  And the Alpine vale below ;
While a thundering torrent near us plunged,
  And the wind-harp murmur'd low.

A châlet, perch'd on the slippery cliff,
  With its patch of tassell'd grain,
Was all that pictured this life's full pulse,
  Her pleasures and weary pain.   ·

I was glad the flowers linger'd still,
  The grass round that threshold clung,
And hands were warm that had tied those sheaves,
  And herbs round that carved roof hung.

For I thought of the days and dreary nights
  In long Winter's cold embrace,
Alps' wildering snows, and shivering drifts—
  And contentment's holy face !

Could anguish venture here, I ask'd,
    Or in mercy pass them by,
Where joys are few, and life is best
    Such stern reality ?

Then I heard her footfall on the snow,
    Through glooms of the forest steal,
The snow in her mantle, the sleet in her hair,
    Her hand for the latch to feel.

I fancied the start of the inmates too,
    And a spectral face at the pane,
The withering tone of a hollow voice,
    Dropping like funeral rain.

I felt her garments freeze as they touch'd,
    The blaze on the hearth-stone quiver,
Then swoon in a column of smoke away,
    And even the darkness shiver !

" What hast thou here for me ?" she ask'd—
    The babe in its cradle started,
She clasp'd it tight, and with icy breath
    And kiss, the frail life parted.

'Twas the kiss of Death, though an angel smiled,
　And lifted the little dust,
To bear it away on wings of love,
　And leave it in God's own trust.

UNDER THE GLACIER.

UNDER the bosom of the snow,
　The calm, unruffled snow,
So still and cold, you could not guess
　What rushes deep below;

A mighty torrent, swift and deep,
　In boiling fury flows
Beneath the blocks of sparkling ice,
　And these deep Alpine snows.

Thus in the pale, transparent face,
　Where neither smile nor tear
Betrays the stormy soul beneath
　That mirror cold and clear;

A mighty torrent, swift and strong,
  Of earnest passion flows,
That wears its channel long and deep,
  To find in death repose.

THE SHADOW ON THE MIST.

THE night stole into the valley,
    And buried the mountains from sight,
There glimmer'd no light in the village,
  Nor one star illumined the night.

At my window I long had been standing
  To hear the wild cataract pour,
As it rush'd through the sombre forest,
  With the burden of death in its roar.

How black grew the darkness around me,
  Which yawn'd like a pitiless grave,
And smote on the mind like those death hours,
  When love, hope, and prayer may not save!

Into this funereal picture
  Roll'd up through the valley a mist,
Like a car it wheel'd swift by my window,
  With a motion no might could resist.

Oh, was it some spirit, some angel,
  With a message to lighten my care?
Till I moved though the shadow still linger'd,
  Then slowly dissolved into air.

Then I moved the light from the table,
  But the shadow had flitted away;
Alas! it was but a reflection—
  'Twas myself in the mist thus astray.

How oft it is thus with life's visions—
  Half the shadows around us we see
Are only the mocking reflections
  Of our own overwrought phantasy!

A NEW MOON.

Dent du Midi, Champery.

THE day crept out of the valley,
　　Entangling his mantle, sun-kiss'd,
In leaves of the grand old forest,
　　To wrap it in shadow and mist.

I sat at my window, long watching
　　For the Queen of night to appear,
The ice-crags above me were shining
　　With the light of her smile on the air.

In fancy I climb'd the high mountain,
　　And there, on its dizziest peak,
On a crag among violet shadows,
　　I found what I went far to seek.

For there lay a crown of bright silver—
    The Queen of the night laid it there—
Its jewels flash'd over the ravine,
    And kindled the dark chasms bare;

Some fell on the froth of the torrent,
    Transforming its bubbles to gems,
Some silver'd the cones of the pine-trees,
    And chisell'd with frost-work the stems;

Some fell on the shrine by the road-side,
    The Virgin seem'd waiting for them,
They set gems in her coronet faded,
    And in the Christ-child's diadem.

The night was all fill'd with moon-glory,
    The nightingale warbled it too,
And the echoes they caught up their lyres,
    And sang this Alp moon-song anew.

AN ASCENT

TO THE SUMMIT OF THE DENT DU MIDI, BY A. B. L. G.
AUG. 7TH, 1866.

EARER to heaven she seem'd to stand
      than earth,
For she had scaled, had reach'd the mountain top;
Dense clouds their vapoury chariots wheel'd
      below,
Though high they look'd to us in valley mists;
The thund'ring torrent roaring at our feet,
To her so high, seem'd only like a thread,
A shimmering thread of broken silver wound
Round the hoar cliffs, and dizzy precipice;
The forest like dwarf'd shrubberies below,
And church's tower, and châlets here and there,
Like children's toys on mimic play-ground
      spread—
All this to her! To us the giddy height
With peril fraught, death's snowy acres vast,
And splinter'd crags o'er precipice of death,
The loosening foothold in the treacherous shale,
The cutting frost-wind and the biting blast,

Death's shafts in threatening stones above her
    slung!
Thus Fancy draws the sketch—I take the glass—
Minute as tiniest insect of the wood,
She starts to sight, her firm hand grasps a
    cross
Which crowns the apex of that mountain's height,
A broken cross, so rudely carved and yet
The symbol sacred.   O beloved cross!
See, now she stoops, beneath its shadow creeps
To find some shelter from the biting blast.
Thus mayst thou climb that higher mount some
    day,
As brave, if on that other Cross thine eye
As steadily is fix'd; if thus, too, grasps
Thy hand, by faith, that other holy Cross
Thy Saviour bore so meekly, long for us,
And when earth's trials and temptations come,
Stand thou as firm a warrior as to-day.
Thus shalt thou need no other Alpen staff,
Nor earthly friend to guide thee on life's way;
Thus plant thy footsteps on that higher Rock,
Where peace, celestial bliss, eternal waits—
That last and grand ascension won—thus mount!

THE ORGAN OF THE PINES.

ARK! to the Organ of the Pines,
　　How it swells through the forest dim,
When Night's weird breeze the mystic keys
　　Awakens to Nature's Hymn.

The Organ of the Pines, how grand!
　　How mysterious the refrain!
So solemnly thrills each cadence soft,
　　Each verse of that glorious strain.

Faint rippling choir of insects, rills,
　　In murmuring minor key,
Lend to the surge of the wailing pines,
　　Their voices in symphony.

How stately the branches bend and sway
　　To the song of " the tuneful choir!"
How they drop their cones like notes released
　　From an orchestra still higher!

For in these forest arches grand,
 Where the winds and the pine trees sing,
The wailing organ bids us list
 To the words that round us wing;

From Nature's own cathedral porch,
 From her transepts and leafy shrines,
What words are these? a *prayer for the dead*,
 With the surging of the pines.

ALPEN FLORA.

OULD'ST thou have a garland of flowers,
 Not forced under tropical glass,
Not pluck'd from the belt of the green sward,
 Nor from gardens through which ye may pass?

Then go to that high Alpine châlet,
 And I'll show you the flowers more fair
Than e'er bloom'd or in grove or in garden,
 Or stifled in close hot-house air.

I'll not fret you with technical titles
    For these children of Alp-land so dear,
With the baptismal dew of God's bounty
    On each leaf, and each petal so clear;

Here are gentians, and orchis, and pinks too,
    With campanula elf-cups that fill,
·Rhododendron and violets regal,
    Meadow-sweet and the rich daffodil.

Such a garland I'll weave for your tresses,
    Which all others shall cast into shade,
Neither crystal nor Sèvres shall ensnare them,
    These smiles on the steep grassy glade;

All wet with the untrampled dew,
    With an odour so sweet and so faint,
Like the memory of loved ones departed,
    Or the prayers of a glorified saint.

It was worth all our climb to the châlet,
    These rare Alpine children to find,
For they dropt from the hands of the Angels,
    Then were sown in the night by the wind.

CLOUD-SCULPTURES.

LAKE LEMAN.

ONE evening we sat together,
  Under the great lime-tree,
As the shadow-king stole softly
From his court of mystery.

The mist had shrouded the mountain,
  Only their outlines dim,
In the spectral light were looming,
  Fantastic in shape and limb.

But the thunder that roll'd above us,
  And trembled within the clouds,
Fill'd those chambers of imagery
  With ghostly shapes and shrouds.

Stretch'd on a couch funereal,
  On a pillow of silver fleece,
A monumental figure grand,
  Form'd a wonderful frontispiece.

It wore the shape of a poet,
    Like Dante stiff and cold,
The grand, stern face in death transfix'd,
    And draped in a shroud of gold.

While round him roll'd black thunder clouds,
    Fantastically piled,
Domes and minarets, strangely mix'd,
    Cloud-sculptures weird and wild!

Primeval birds, and elfin sprites,
    And ghosts in winding-sheets,
With outstretch'd arms, in vapour draped,
    And monks in still retreats.

Gnomes and demons, sprites and fays,
    Whirl'd in a giddy dance—
A waltz of shadows quaint, bizarre,
    Finish'd th' extravagance.

Then came dark Night in widow's weeds,
    Broke up the spectral dance,
Buried from sight the poet grand,
    And ended the eve's romance.

THE ANGELUS.

THE rain is filling the valley,
   Dripping from crag and from châlet,
The chimes for the "Angelus" ringing,
The angels are calling and singing
                    To prayer!

Yes, the angels call us to prayer,
On Jesu to lay all our care,
Oh list to the "Angelus" ringing,
Oh list to the angels soft singing
                    To prayer!

THE MAID OF SAVOY.

O girlish and fair, with her golden hair,
   And a step as light as the noiseless air,
With a voice as soft as the wooing leaves,
Kiss'd fondly at night when the zephyr grieves,
      Was the Maid of Savoy.

Like pictures we see by that holy friar,
Whose pencil he dipp'd in devotion's fire,
When angels, and saints, and Christ's martyrs
    dead,
Started back into life on his canvas' thread—
      This the Maid of Savoy.

As saintly as ever " Fra Beato" drew,
And purer than snow, or the harebell's dew,
Ay, calmer than moon-kiss'd Leman was she,
This daughter of Chillon of noble degree,
      And Maid of Savoy.

Whether in minuet stately she moved,
How sad was her mien,—or careless she roved
Around the old castle and battlements drear,
Weaving pale violets in her gold hair—
    Sweet Maid of Savoy.

Or tuning her rebeck to sad even-song,
Luring the linnets from shadows among,
Or on the high terrace, where lonely she sat
Watching the nightfall, and gloom-whirling bat—
    Sad Maid of Savoy.

Or musing on Alp-kings that round her home
  frown'd,
In their mantles of snow by pine forests crown'd;
Or climbing in fancy those gall'ries of ice,
So recklessly hung on the sheer precipice—
    Dream'd the Maid of Savoy.

Or on crags where the chamois, cunning as fleet,
Can scarce find a foothold or path for her feet;
Or lower down still, where the vine grapes of Vaud,
On sun-loving slopes, bud, blossom, and grow
    For the Maid of Savoy.

Her thought was of him in his dungeon so deep,
Under the castle's black, fortified keep—
A martyr for freedom, who paced his stone square,
Once priest, now Reformer, the stern Bonnivard—
           Sighed Maid of Savoy.

Six summers he had to that ring been enchain'd,
Till youth, hope, and life had utterly waned ;
Like a warrior in death-wound Europe then
        quiver'd,
The cry was, " The faith to the saints once de-
        livered ! "
           It reach'd the Maid of Savoy.

But he was the sorrow that shrouded her youth,
The thorn in her peace, the doubt in all truth ;
And each mountain breeze that o'er her Alps came,
Bore sighs from that prisoner, and Bonnivard's
        name
           To the Maid of Savoy.

THE SHADOW OF CHÂSTELLARD.

PART I.

Clarens.

LOOMS the Castle on the height,
Whistling winds in wayward flight,
Sweep the turret with their might—
      Proud Châstellard.

High above the stormy lake,
Whose waves on Chillon's fortress break—
None e'er again shall cheer partake
      In Châstellard.

Grim old portraits deck the wall,
And threadbare tapestries down fall,
In banquet rooms, and silent hall
      Of Châstellard.

Voices whisper of the dead,
The dance, the song, the loved, the wed,
Black coffin palls, and last tears shed
      At Châstellard.

Sad symphony of other days,
Quaint minstrelsy of ancient lays,
The wizard touch of Time betrays—
      Grim Châstellard.

A turret on the western flank,
With ivy grown, and weeds too rank
To prate of sunshine, falls a-blank
      On Châstellard.

It scowls down on a rocky ledge,
Where hawks hide sullen in the sedge,
And scream upon the ragged hedge,
      Round Châstellard.

There silence speaks of days gone by,
Of maiden fair, of history,
Hinting some tale of mystery
      Of Châstellard.

For in that turret grim and old,
Wrapt in her mantle's woof of gold,
Once sat, long sat in shivering cold,
      A bride at Châstellard.

Long watch'd she, waited, only said,
" Why tarrieth he, so lately wed ? "
Ah, well-a-day ! the dead, the dead
    Haunt Châstellard.

Say a mass for the wanderer's soul—
Mutter'd a monk beneath his cowl,
Nor heeded she that 'dismal dole,
    At Châstellard.

Ah, well-a-day ! ah, well-a-day !
The tarnish'd gold and silver grey
Of bridal shreds and youth's decay,
    At Châstellard.

PART II.

THE hawk skims through the frosty air,
Like some dark demon of despair,
Nor fixes e'en his startled stare
    On bride of Châstellard.

o

For down below that turret's base,
A deep black shadow sinks apace,
Even the violets will not grace
   The shadow of Châstellard.

For ever it stains the sickly grass,
The sunlight never that way doth pass,
For ever, for ever, the shadow, alas!
   That haunts old Châstellard.

The shadow of a bride just wed,
Yet never a wife, and every shred
Of nuptial robe to winds long sped—
   From tower of Châstellard.

Two hundred years the tower has swept,
Two hundred years the rains have wept
Over that shadow, and sun has crept
   In vain round Châstellard.

But now a baron glooms alone,
Here with his daughter still unwon,
Her beauty now like southern sun
   Re-lights old Châstellard.

Now wandereth she at sunny noon,
Now loitereth she by fickle moon,
Now waits to watch the shadows swoon
    Around grim Châstellard ;

Now lures the ivy o'er this spot,
And fosters rosemary in that plot,
Now twines the wall-fruit, apricot,
    O'er th' shadow of Châstellard.

In vain, in vain,—'tis ever there,—
Distraught the dress, and wind-toss'd hair,
Ah, well-a-day ! forsaken Fair,
    That maid of Châstellard !

For while the shadow there doth lie,
The curse of Châstellard must vie
With maid unwed that there must die,
    Who blooms at Châstellard.

Her songs the echoes deaf may wake,
Her tears her harp-strings rust, and break,
While still she vainly prays, " Oh take
    This curse from Châstellard!"

May plant the rosemary and thyme,
And strive in fortitude sublime,
To coax that shadow ere her prime
      Shall wane on Châstellard.

The rose from off her cheek must fade,
And gold grow dim in tress and braid,
Her eyes lose light from tears long shed,
      Long shed at Châstellard.

Let tears drop o'er the clambering rose,
And the last broken lattice close
In that doom'd turret's drear repose—
      Lone Châstellard.

This is the legend of the tower,
Of th' maid who ne'er forsook her bower,
But watch'd and waited hour to hour
      At Châstellard.

THE AVE.

WENT to my church one evening,
　　As the Ave was ringing clear,
To my forest-church, my favourite shrine,
　　Under firs, by the torrent near.

Sublime was that grand interior!
　　So far from earth's noise and din,
With that aureate dome cerulean,
　　Where the angels enter in.

And those living columns round me,
　　Of the stately spruce and pine,
Rearing masses of Gothic arches,
　　Leaf-traceries to entwine.

I fancied windows round me,
　　All brilliant with stainèd glass,
And saints here in glory shining,
　　As waiting for us to pass.

Then came the peal from the torrent,
　With the chanting of voices rare,
And the tracery thrill'd above me
　To the swell of the heavenly air.

It was Nature's own " Te Deum,"
　All join'd that Pæan true,
As it rose and swell'd on the mystic air,
　Then died in the dreamy blue.

I look'd around—was I dreaming?
　For underneath my feet
Bright flowers, and pine-cones were mingled,
　And the odour was damp and sweet.

But my church was only a forest,
　Each column a stately pine,
My seat but a stump all moss-grown,
　The windows of Heaven's design!

For through the tracery broken,
　Came the sun with his pencil keen,
And here and there with his magic touch,
　Left pictures where he had been.

At length my reverie ended,
    In my church in a grove of pine,
For this had been my cathedral,
    And this my forest shrine.

SUNSET AT THE "PORTE DU SOLEIL."

Morgens.

THE Painter of the sky threw down
    His palette rich and rare;
It caught upon this lower world,
    And made it passing fair!

With pencil dipp'd in rainbow tints,
    He pencill'd leaf and stem
Of spruce, and fir, and giant oaks,
    In hues that mock'd the gem.

He touch'd the rocks and shelving cliffs,
    And in the wimpling stream,
He drew in gold his image fair,
    Bewitching as a dream.

He lit the spire, and gilt the cross,
    Then dash'd a flood of tint
On the church windows' dusty panes,
    Till they were all a-glint.

An artist at his easel sat,
    To sketch this picture fair ;
But ere his palette tints were mix'd,
    He dropp'd it in despair.

For the stealthy form of Night drew near,
    And that fair picture stole,
Nor left the grand original,
    Art's conquests to enroll.

But I fancy 'twas the last attempt
    This artist ever made,
To copy from that picture grand—
    That sun-lit pallisade.

A FROST PICTURE ON A WINDOW.

Montanvert.

ON the window's frosty pane,
  The fickle moon is shining;
Silv'ring groves of fir and pine,
  The Frost-king's own designing.

Wandering rillets lock'd in ice,
  And woodland footpaths winding,
Into mysteries fancy wove,
  The Frost-king's own reminding.

Distant hills in frozen mist,
  And spangled shrubs low bending,
Caves befringed with icicles,
  And stars their lanterns lending;

Cheating us on a window pane
  With pictures brightly gleaming;
Till the sun shall swift dispel,
  And find us only dreaming.

MOON-LIGHT.

QUEEN of the Alpine night!
　　Smile from thy cloudy height,
Fling down thy jewels bright
　　　On forest and stream.

Blossoms of silver drop
Down on this icy slope,
Light up the crags to hope,
　　　As gloomy they frown.

Jewel the cascades foam,
Light the cathedral dome,
Lift from its shadow-tomb,
　　　The death-precipice.

Filigree moonlight woo,
Châlets and valleys too,
Bright in thy silver glow,
　　　To Him lift our hearts!

THE FLOWER CHORUS.

TO MRS. Γ. C. B.

FROM the crowns of the angels we dropp'd,
  Our gems in earth's valleys to sow,
And where their faint footsteps have stopp'd,
  We awake, and our chorus bestow.

With the saints too we lie down to sleep,
  And weave o'er the shrouds of the blest;
Sing plaintive—their memories weep,
  As we wander and bloom o'er their rest.

Our prelude at dawn we renew,
  Our chorus, full chorus at morn,
Fold our hands when the twilight's soft dew
  Drips o'er the sun's gold-shatter'd urn.

From the crowns of the angels we dropp'd,
  And were sown in the night by the wind,
And where each faint footstep has stopp'd,
  We hallow each track thus enshrined.

Still softly our chorus we sing,
    And mingle our voices where'er
Sharp discords of earth harshly ring,
    And fill all earth's wastes with our prayer.

Just fancy your world without flowers !
    Can you guess what a bier it would prove,
And how much joy you owe in life's hours
    To our day-dream of beauty and love ?

What thoughts, unexpress'd and half-ripe,
    What yearnings in love's golden hours,
That could ne'er ripple up to the lip,
    Pleaded softly in language of flowers.

E'en our ghosts too are often enshrined,
    All faded and scentless and dead,
With some vow or some day-dream entwined
    With a love-song as quick away sped.

Round the cross, and the shrine too, we cling,
    And love to breathe life away there,
Round the altar to bud and to wing
    Our perfume with incense of prayer.

Thus list to the chorus we sing,
    So varied each voice is, so sweet,
Nor scorn e'en one lesson we bring,
    Though thrown by a rose at your feet.

For we spring from earth's dust to aspire,
    Our chorus we sing as we rise,
Till, caught by the angels, still higher
    It mounts to the blue of the skies.

INTERRUPTED BY A ROUNDELAY OF ROSES.

        BORN in June,
            Deck'd a bride,
        Wreathed her brow,
            Girdle tied.

        Loop'd her robe,
            Caught her veil,
        Clasp'd her hand
            At altar rail.

Sing we then,
　　Roses reign,
Glory brief,
　　Short campaign.

Roses, roses,
　　Summer's story,
Shadows lighting
　　Summer's glory.

Petals opening,
　　Petals flying,
Petals shutting,
　　Petals dying.

Roses blowing,
　　Roses falling,
Roses fading,
　　Roses calling.

Roses old,
　　Roses new,
Often twining
　　With the rue.

THE FLOWER CHORUS.

Bridal roses,
　Briefest glory,
Summer roses,
　Sad their story.

Autumn roses,
　Winter roses,
Thus our chorus
　Plaintive closes.

THE WILD-FLOWERS SING.

WE breathe our lay, our mystic hymn,
　Sweet octaves from untrodden bowers,
From shady haunts, from fissures dim,
　We sing our reign, the woodland flowers.

When stands the veilèd bride so fair
　At altar-step, for blessing given
Upon a life she hopes may wear
　Some flower-hues of happier heaven;

We sometimes mingle in her veil, .
 And woodland blossoms bind her wreath,
While tenderly our lives exhale
 In transient but impassion'd breath.

Or sleeps in coffin'd night the dead,
 All still, we hallow earth's loved dust,
And grow unbidden where ye tread,
 We wild-flowers ling'ring there in trust.

Thus smile we on life's saddest hours,
 Exiled from heaven we light earth's dream,
We woodland flowers, wild woodland flowers,
 Breathe Nature in her holiest gleam.

When music's spell in silence dies,
 When pleasure's phantoms count but hours,
When wreathed smiles but fade in sighs,
 And dancing feet crush wither'd flowers.

Then waft we still our sweetest breath,
 Though cull'd at morn, to die at eve,
Nor vain our life, nor vain our death,
 If one sweet lesson we may leave.

A Rose Geranium sings.

You may crush us and break us at will,
  But forgiveness may hide in a grief;
Forgiveness! sweet unction of fragrance,
  Bruised from a geranium leaf.

You may cherish us too when we're dead,
  All wither'd, forgot, in some book,
Yet we'll waft you the scent of old bye-gones,
  If you ever by chance on us look.

We'll bring back that long-vanish'd day-dream—
  Now don't look so grave and severe
If Time's finger points to a wrinkle,
  Or a silver lock hides there or here!

Alas! what a long agone season—
  Almost a tradition—you smile!
When this spray was once freshly blooming,
  And cherish'd in happy exile!

P

The record of one moon-tryst glory,
  Once worn next your heart in a leaf
All folded in rose-tinted paper,
  That breathed but a Nightingale's grief.

Alas! 'tis a very old story,
  We are dead—and e'en love will estrange;
But hark to the chorus of insects—
  The burthen is evermore—Change!

INSECT CHOIR.

WE hum in the day when the sunbeams play
Among laughing leaves and the flowers' brief
        sway,
Down dipping our wings in the rills of gold,
Which flow with the sunbeams down on the wold.

All arm'd too we are in our bright array,
With swords and with darts for the wood affray,
E'en beetles wear cuirasses bronzèd bright,
And the dragon-fly, stately as armour'd knight;

We court the bright sunbeams, but hide in the
    night,
We have nothing to do with the cold starlight,
But rest in leaf-palaces, hid in the bowers,
To be folded to sleep in the hearts of the flowers.

You think we've no mission perhaps to perform,
We legion of insects that round you oft swarm :
But we've not lived in vain, I know you will say,
If we've praised our Creator but one summer-
    day.

But hark to the sunbeams ! their carol they sing,
So much we owe them for the gold on each wing,
For bronzing our cuirasses, burnish'd so bright,
To mirror the roses that clasp us at night.

CAROL OF SUNBEAMS.

Ay, glance we, dance we,
    True artists we are,
Gilding the pictures
    That shadows ensnare.

Mingling our colours
   On palettes of light
Caught from the rainbow,
   Or cloud of the night.

Painting at evening,
   When the vase of the sun
Lies shatter'd, broken,
   With day's glory gone.

Catching each fragment,
   To gild leaf and flower,
Gold-fringing the shadows
   That drape the night-hour.

Ay, spin we, weave we,
   True artists we are,
Carrying our pencils
   Gold-tipp'd in the air.

So frail are we sunbeams
   To vie with the flowers,
Or sing in their chorus
   The song of the hours.

THE FLOWER CHORUS.

Though we paint every petal,
  And gild every spray,
Thus aiding their chorus
  Our own sunny way.

But hark now to the hours !
  They sing as they fly,
Though our carol of sunbeams
  With twilight must die.

THE SONG OF THE HOURS.

A SHADOWY band are we,
  Sing flying, flying !
One brush of our robes astray,
  Hear roses sighing !

A shadowy band are we,
  Sing passing, passing !
A touch of our light array,
  Zephyrs surpassing.

Roses blow, roses go,
Sing fading, fading,
If the last of the floating band
Comes rudely shading.

Roses drop, roses die,
Sing dying, dying,
Only the flowers count by hours,
Sing flying, flying!

A shadowy band are we,
Sing changing, ranging;
There is only one sun-dial true,
One lyre rings unchanging.

WILLOWS WEEPING.

WILLOWS weeping, willows weeping
O'er the streamlet, bubbles reaping;
Only bubbles for their keeping,
Giddy bubbles, bubbles sweeping.

Willows drooping, willows stooping
　　Over urns where bays are grouping,
Funeral urns but ashes cooping,
　　Willows, willows, drooping, drooping!

Willows weep o'er streamlets brawling,
　　Nature's mourners,—grief enthralling;
Willows weeping—leaf-tears falling
　　O'er the grave where we stand calling.

THE LAY OF THE GLADIÒLUS.

GLADIÒLI! Gladiòli!
Sing your lay, all sweet and holy,
Sheathe your daggers in the glade,
'Mid the daisies hide each blade,
Matchless hilts of glowing lilies,
Brighter than the daffodillies,
Upward from each blade thus climbing,
To our chorus lend your rhyming.

Gladiòli! Gladiòli!
Summer's pride, and summer's wholly,

For the shadow-king's own warfare,
With spectral armies of the night air ;
Dewy copse and glade thus haunting,
And the day-king ever daunting,
Sing your lay all sweet and holy,
Gladiòli! Gladiòli!

Gladiòli! Gladiòli!
Point your allegory holy,
Sheathe your daggers in the belt
Of the green-sward—ye have dealt
Your moral, that forgiveness may
Sheathe a dagger in a fray;
Thus to breathe your lay all holy,
Gladiòli! Gladiòli!

Gladiòli! Gladiòli!
One more word to point more fully,—
Daggers of detraction never,
Nor envy's tongue can really sever
Truth from falsehood, for I ween
The motive oft is clearly seen;
Such daggers may be flower-hilted,
With Heav'n's bright blossoms never wilted,

If Christ's sweet patience—that meek flower—
Blooms fragrant in the heart's cold hour,
And such lessons make us lowly,
Gladiòli! Gladiòli!

THE LILY.

VIRGIN Lily, silver gleaming,
Lift thy veil, reveal thy dreaming;
Emblem of the Holy Virgin,
In thy stately grace, immerge in
Rippling dew-drops, thy white splendour,
Wash'd so pure, thou sweet Defender!
From the nettles round thee growing,
From the hemlock round thee blowing,
Thus towering upward, queenly flower,
In thy stately grace and power,
Upward from thy flaunting compeers,
Wand'ring 'mid the weeds and wild tares,
Emblem in thy holy splendour
Of the pure life we should render
Back to Him who proved your glory
Greater than a king's life story—

" E'en Solomon who in his pride,
And glory too, was not arrayed
Like one of these."—O Lily fair !
O Queen of flowers, hear our prayer !

  *   *   *   *

Thus the chorus of flowers
 And the roses' brief lay,
With the song of the hours,
 Float softly away.

The insects' soft humming,
 And geraniums' grief,
The plaint of the willow,
 And wild flowers brief,

All carol the story
 So sadly and sweet;
Sing on then, O chorus !
 Your day-dream complete.

  *   *   *   *

For from crowns of the angels ye fell,
 And were sown by the wind in the sod,
Your mission is ended, ye've sung
 Your chorus, O flowers ! to God.

CHORAL PHRASES.

" The Holy Church throughout all the world doth
acknowledge Thee."

Te Deum.

THE SHIP.

BESIDE the ocean's shelving lip I stood,
    Watching the billows in the distance
        break ;
How idly flapp'd the sails in anchored crafts,
How bright the beacon's tongue lick'd up the
        surf !
There standing on a drift of weed I mused,—
So crisp it was from sun and wand'ring wave
Which raked the heaps, and sprinkled them with
        shells,
And limpets clinging to the Algæ fast.
Thus stands the Christian pilgrim by the shore—
That mystic shore which bounds the future life—
Where like Christ's watchman list'ning to the
        night,

He marks the Church, the battle ship of Faith,
Riding majestic through the surging deep;
Though splintered be her masts, and bulwarks
      wreck'd,
And sails in tatters torn before the gale,
Yet on she floats, her rudder safely mann'd
By Him the Captain of Salvation's hosts;
Through the dim mists one beacon ever shines,
And distant on the far horizon looms
Its steadfast and unfailing star of hope.
Come persecution, bitterness, and woe,
Still floats she on—Christ's Apostolic ship,
Her destiny the port of Heaven to reach,
Her anchor dropp'd in Heaven's eternal calms.

THE HOLY CATHOLIC CHURCH.

TO S. F. A. C.

OOK on thy Bride, O Lord,
  Thy Bride, the Church in her captivity ;
Each fetter snap, each golden link restore,
  That mars her unity.

Thy spotless Bride, the Church,
  As in the early Apostolic day,
When glow'd the light upon her altars, e'en
  Through persecution's sway.

That Light that never waned,
  When all was darkest then the brighter shone,
That cheer'd each steadfast heart, and led the way
  Where shines th' Eternal Throne.

Look on thy Bride, O Lord,
  Thy Bride the Church, in her captivity ;
Lift up her veil, that all the world may see
  Her truth and majesty.

BY THE SEA OF GALILEE.

"PEACE!" whisper o'er these sacred shores,
　　Sad waves of Galilee;
Naught save the wild birds' plaintive cry
　　Profanes the melody.
An ancient convent shelves the brink—
　　O sea! where breezes moan—
Weaving dim shadows o'er those waves,
　　Of Him who walk'd here lone.

Sad echoes of the world's great Light,
　　That Light which once here shone,
That dawn'd upon a guilty world,
　　In sin's dark night o'erthrown.
Mount Hermon's glittering shield of ice,
　　Breastplate of virgin snow,
Rears its proud height in majesty
　　O'er solemn wastes below.

Divinely sweet, though sadly sad,
  To wander here alone,
To feel the withering blight that rests
  On hill, on plain, on stone ;
Where He once taught " the Way, the Truth,"
  Here whisper'd, " Peace, be still,"
Here calm'd the tempest by His voice,
  Subdued the heart's proud will ;

When all was beautiful and fair,
  The olive and the vine
Luxuriant girdling hill and vale
  Of sacred Palestine !
But now the Bedouin haunts the shores,
  His black tent stains the sward,
Fierce sons of Ismael dwell here now,
  A lawless, barbarous horde.

But " lilies of the field" still bloom,
  And breathe faint odours sweet
O'er scenes once hallow'd by His love,
  Trod by His sacred feet.

Q

But not alone I paced thy shores,
    O Galilean Lake !
Hearing the wild-fowls' plaintive cry
    The holy silence break.

A pilgrim though, but not alone
    Was I beside that sea,
When came the whisper, " Peace be still,"
    " My peace I give to thee."
I heard that voice, I felt that touch
    I ask'd for nothing more,
But kiss'd my pilgrim's staff, and wept
    Beside that rippling shore.

Tiberias.

THE MARTYR AGES.

"The noble army of Martyrs praise Thee."

DOWN the shadowy Past they float,
    Procession calm and grand,
With shining robes, with crowns of gold,
    Palms in each outstretch'd hand.

Thus walk they now with Him in white,
   That great and ransom'd throng,
Christ's martyr'd saints, whose voices swell
   The everlasting song.

Adown Time's shadowy cloisters dim,
   These saints of earth's renown
Still bear to us the words of hope,
   " Thy cross must win Thy crown."

Each holy face looks down on us
   As if in pity bent,
Each branch of palm, each crown of gold,
   Speak words so eloquent !

That burning stake, nor torturing rack,
   Nor persecution's sword,
Are now the tests in this our day
   Of service to our Lord.

But patience, gentleness, and love,
   In works of mercy shown,
Renunciation of the will
   For His true Will alone.

Thus Faith, and Hope, and Charity,
   From Him now heavenward come,
To teach us here to win the palm
   And crown' of martyrdom.

TRUST.

O God I lift my heart in praise,
   To God I wing my prayer,
No hour is sad, no day is dark,
   If Thou, my Christ, art there.

No cup too bitter then to drain,
   No loneliness too lone,
No pain too wearisome to bear,
   Since all by Him is known.

No doubting plaint, no anxious dread,
   No murmuring question " Why ? "
" The Lord hath done it," rest my soul
   On Him eternally.

A HYMN FOR CONFIRMATION.

AKE Thou my heart, my Saviour, all be
    Thine,
My every thought I consecrate to Thee;
What are life's joys and fading dreams at best,
Compared with perfect bliss eternally?

That restful rest, in life's perplexing cares,
That peaceful peace, which but in Thee is found.
That trust triumphant anchor'd on the Cross
Once borne when Night and Death on Calvary
    frown'd.

How shadowy seem life's fading dreams at best,
How brief her trials, disappointments, woes,
How lightly tread we earth's bewildering maze,
With heaven before us, and her long repose.

Take then my heart, my Saviour, all be Thine,
My life, my death, I consecrate to Thee :
Only one prayer I breathe, that in return
Thou wilt, my Saviour, give Thyself to me.

"A Pilgrim and a Sojourner as all my Fathers were."

HERE then I have no country,
  No fix'd, no steady gleam,
Here I am a pilgrim still,
  A wanderer in a dream.

Here then I tread on shadows,
  Life's bridge from shadows spun,
From floating mists that vanish swift
  Before the race is won.

Here all is fleeting, transient,
  Vague as a feverish dream,
The brightest joys, like rainbow hues,
  Fade in a sickly gleam.

There only is my country,
　Where I shall no more roam
When Death shall take my pilgrim's staff,
　And call the wanderer home.

And there where life's dark shadows
　Shall fade in eternal sun,
And where sweet rest shall come at last,
　When life's brief race is won.

Thus to the world then dying,
　To its phantoms and its cares,
Through Faith I see the silver wheat
　Shine now amid the tares.

There then I have my country,
　Where I shall no more roam
When death shall take my pilgrim's staff,
　And call the wanderer home.

GUARDIAN ANGELS.

" He giveth His angels charge concerning thee."

OH, ye who watch us night and day,
And round about our pathway glide,
Help us to love, to watch, to pray,
Lest our frail footsteps swerve or slide.

Oh, ye celestial spirits bright,
Who watch beside us night and day,
Guard us from our eternal foe,
And guide us lest we go astray.

Spread your bright wings, and shelter give,
With noiseless footfall linger near,
Shield us from foes without, within,
And keep us safe from year to year.

How oft we've wander'd, turn'd aside,
Nor heard the gentle footfall near,
Nor the sweet voice, " With Him abide,
With Him, your Saviour, ever here.

" He gives us charge concerning thee,
    To keep thee from dark evil's snare,
Abide in faith, and lowly wait,
    Guarded by faith's best corselet—prayer.

" Unseen, unheard, we patient wait,
    Our Master sends us, we are His,
He gives us charge concerning thee,
    To help thee heavenward where He is.

" We screen thee oft from danger's fear,
    We draw thee oft to secret prayer,
Though still unconscious ye may be,
    Your guardian angel sojourns near."

Oh ye who watch us night and day !
    Blest spirits rest where'er we stray,
If dark the path, if sharp the stones,
    Then lead us in the happier way,

And softly sing celestial hymns,
    To Christ we love tune all your wires,
And let us join our feeble strains
    To anthems of celestial choirs.

FOR WHITSUNTIDE.

" Awake O Northwind and come thou South, blow upon my
garden, that the spices thereof may flow out."

Canticles.

WAKE O Northwind! come thou South,
   Blow on this garden fair,
That Love's sweet spices may exhale
   And wake the lifeless air.

Revive the dying flowers, that still
   About her borders live,
Breathe on their petals in the dust,
   Love's dew in mercy give.

Come to Thy garden, Lord of Light!
   Thy Church's bowers so fair,
Dispel each cloud that hides the sight
   Of Thy great Presence there.

Come Thou dear Sunlight of the soul,
   Each drooping spirit raise
From shadows of earth's twilight dim,
   From frosts of faithless days.

That every path may reach that shrine,
   The altar of Thy grace,
Where faith's undying flame ne'er wanes,
   But lights the sacred place.

That every flower may turn to Thee,
   From error's cold and night,
Shoot forth its feeble tendrils, clasp,
   And live again in light.

In Sacramental light and life,
   O mystery unspoken !
Come to Thy garden, Lord of Light,
   Revive the flowers broken.

Each countless blade of grass, ay, weeds,
   Rank in neglected bowers,
Revive to life through Thy great love,
   And change these weeds to flowers.

" Awake then, Northwind, come thou South,"
   Come from those bowers of spice,
Come to the Church Christ planted here
   To bloom in Paradise.

" LIGHT OF THE WORLD."

FOR HOLY COMMUNION.

IGHT of the World!" we bow to Thee,
And at Thine Altar bend the knee,
To seek Communion, calm, and blest,
In perfect union, perfect rest.

The Angel-guardians linger here,
While softly float their garments near,
And visions of celestial bowers
Steal o'er these Sacramental hours.

The tapers' glow, symbolic light
Of Him, the sun of earth's sad night,
Bid darkness at His presence flee—
" Light of the World," we worship Thee!

And breathe your mystic hymn, sweet flowers,
Though silent as these lips of ours,
When at the Altar of His grace,
He lifts the veil, reveals His face.

O Bread of Angels ! Feast of Heaven !
O Wine of Life, by Jesu given !
Here on the Altar of His grace,
Behold the solemn Sacrifice.

O manna in life's wilderness !
The food of angels, kiss of peace,
Visions of Home, yet earth's rare gem.
Jerusalem, Jerusalem !

A HYMN FOR THE HOLY COMMUNION.

FOREST cloisters, yield your flowers !
And consecrate these royal hours,
Let prayer's sweet incense, upward rise,
  With Love's faint whispers to the skies.

O Son of Mary, Jesu sweet !
  Our hearts are yearning Thee to greet,
Come in Thy glory softly near,
  Reveal Thy presence to us here.

O Son of Mary, Saviour mine !
  Thou who hast call'd Thyself "the Vine,"
Poor wither'd branches though we be,
  Incorporate with Thyself are we.

We come adoring, lowly kneel,
  The chalice waits our lips to seal,
O Bread of Life ! O mystic Wine !
  Revive these wither'd branches—Thine.

Not wholly dead, if sear'd and dry,
  O blessed vast reality !
Still are we branches of that " Vine,"
  Through Sacramental feast divine.

O beatific vision blest !
  O wondrous love ! O peaceful rest !
O Thou the Life, the Truth, the " Vine,"
  Revive these wither'd branches—Thine.

VIA CRUCIS.

FOR GOOD FRIDAY.

IN that lonely dreary way,
  Where the shades of darkness stray,
  Meek beneath a traitor's sting,
  Bow'd before an earthly king—
            Our Jesus Lord.

Mock'd, reviled, and thrice denied,
With the guilty crucified,
Son of Mary, thus for me
The crucified on Calvary—
                    Our Jesus Lord.

Let my tears in anguish flow,
Let my head dejected bow,
Oh, let me find Thy Cross but bliss,
And whisper—O what love was this,
                    Our Jesus Lord!

And for all Thy love and grace,
Calvary's cross and Death's embrace,
And that plaint of agony—
My God, hast Thou forsaken me?
                    O Jesus Lord!

Jesu! on this solemn day
We follow Thee! O mournful way!
Ours the shame, the Cross to bear,
Ours the crown of thorns to wear,
                    Blest Jesus Lord.

MATER DOLOROSA.

BY the Cross her watch still keeping,
　　In those vigils nought could stir,
When night's dews were o'er Him weeping,
　　In the lonely sepulchre,

Stood sweet Mary sad, forsaken,
　　Pale with weeping, watching, woe,
Now her Dearest from her taken,
　　Laid in Joseph's garden low.

Faint with anguish, grief unspoken,
　　O that drear tremendous night,
When o'erhung the heights of Calvary,
　　The wrath of God, the Infinite!

Lone upon that rocky summit
　　Stood the Cross, the sacred Sign,
Streaming with the sacred blood-drops,
　　Where He hung, the Lord divine.

Holy Virgin, lonely, weeping,—
  See her tears bedew the sod,
Mourning for a dying nation,
  A world that would not know its God;

Till cold dawn o'er Calvary breaking,
  Through the clouds pale sunlight crept,
Pierced the blackness, breathed faint comfort—
  Still the Virgin-mother wept.

A FUNERAL HYMN.

" Planted in His likeness."

OWN in weakness,—raised in power,
  Sown in dust, in sorrow, sin,
Sown the mortal, raised immortal,
  Incorruption thus to win.

" Dust to dust,"—to ashes render'd,
  Inglorious seed in ruin sown,
But from the germ a heav'nly flower
  Now in Paradise hath blown.

And the earthly vase, though broken,
    Scatter'd in the mould must lie,
Yet it held a germ immortal,
    Blossoming now beyond the sky.

Thus death only sows these blossoms
    Where the little children tread,
And the stately yew perennial,
    Solemn guards the peaceful dead.

AN EASTER HYMN.

AWAKE! awake! put on thy strength—
    Thy strength O Zion, sing!
The Lord is risen, rise with Him,
    And hail our Easter King.

Mark how the Light on Judah's hills
    Lifts the death glooms of night;
Behold your Sun of Righteousness,
    Behold your Lord of Light!

Our Lenten fasting, mourning o'er,
   Our world without her King—
O Grave, where is thy victory now?
   O Death, where is thy sting?

The Sun has dawned upon our night—
   Ring, chimes of Easter, ring!
And praiseful anthems rise and swell,
   To hail our risen King.

Let sorrow's voice be soothed to rest,
   Pale mourners, blossoms bring,
And deck the grave, 'tis now the shrine
   Where rose our Easter King!

Beside that grave, beneath His Cross,
   Earth's sufferings meekly lay,
Triumphant sing our risen King,
   And welcome Easter Day.

"At evening time it shall be light."—*Zec.* ziv. 7.

NOT day, nor night, "not clear, nor dark"—
Thus sang the Prophet in fore-
shadow'd night,
Sang of the Light to fall on Judah's hills,
"At evening time it shall be light."

Then came the Light! and darkness fled,
As ages lapsed, and wheel'd their reckless flight,
The Prophet slept in death, but not his words,
"At evening time it shall be light."

Oft as life's shadows gather round,
And clouds adrift obscure the moonless night,
He softly whispers to the faintest heart,
"At evening time it shall be light."

Thus evening falls when death draws near,
When life is ebbing, softly folds the night,
The dying hear when all to us is dark,
"At evening time it shall be light."

Apostles, ministers of Christ,
Can only lead souls to that mystic Gate,
There leave them, for the paradise beyond,
 When even-tide brings them " the light."

For not at glow of noon-tide sun,
Nor yet in blaze of giddy hours most bright,
No, not till all of earth wanes dim and pale,
 Shall " evening time " bring us " the light."

Love then must fold her drooping wings,
And veil her face, for mark how wondrous bright,
How passing radiant is that room of death,
 Which brings the dying Christian " light."

Dim shadows of the Great Beyond
Shroud us—for him, no more the feud, the fight ;
Christ's warrior sleeps ! while angels round him
  sing—
 " At evening time it shall be light."

O glorious prospect, thus to wait,
As glooms earth's waning shadows on the sight,
Faith's taper light ! O live, the promise wait—
 " At evening time it shall be light."

PERFECT DAY.

" And there shall be no night *there."*

WHEN days are dark, and nights are drear,
Forlorn and cold, no haven near,
Guide Thou my feet, make Thou my way,
And turn my darkest night to day.

Guide me, O guide me to that shore
Where sin and pain are known no more,
Where no dark days, and no more night,
Shall hide Thy presence from my sight.

If days are dark, and nights are drear,
Forlorn and cold, no haven near,
Trust thou in God, be sure His way
Shall lead thee to the perfect day.

AN EARLY CHRISTIAN MARTYR.

(A Picture by Paul de la Roche.)

ADOWN Death's weary river lone she drifts,
  The night glooms black, the tide runs
    swift and deep,
Faintly the glimm'ring stars above her shine,
  And o'er her watery couch their vigils keep.

The martyr's crown lights up the silv'ry wake,
  Peaceful and happy, on death's wave she lies,
The night will wane, and early morning break
  For her, and she will wake in paradise.

Serene she sleeps on death's remorseless flood,
  Nought now to her the night, the cold, the
    tides,
Her arms are folded on her peaceful breast,
  As onward to the haven calm she glides.

Hark! angels singing, hovering in her wake,
 Softly they whisper, " Sister spirit blest,
Thy martyr's cross at length has won thy crown,
 And thou hast enter'd into perfect rest."

For her no darkness now, where all is light,
 For her no torturing rack, no prison bars,
Death's tide has only borne her swiftly home,
 And now " she lives in peace beyond the
  stars." *

FLOWERS ON THE ALTAR.

To E. T. H.

THE blossoms, Lord, more sweetly grow,
 That round thine Altar bud and blow,
 In this great calm, this heavenly air
 Breathing devotion, love and prayer.

---

 * Inscription on a martyr's tomb in the Basilica of St. Agnese.
Rome.

Dim is the light by shadows spun—
Here, think you, pine they for the sun,
Or rains of heaven, or dews of night,
Or earth's sad sod to bloom more bright?

O no—for angels tend them here,
They love the church's atmosphere,
Blossoms so fragrant, earth's true gems,
Just dropt from seraph's diadems.

So let the flowers live and grow,
And round His Altar bud and blow,
The incense of their bloom to rise
With our faint prayers to Paradise.

A HYMN FOR ALL SAINTS.

INSCRIBED TO THE REV. ARCHER GURNEY.

PEAL we the anthem grand!
  Through the arches, hark! it rolls,
The tide of praise, from heart and voice,
  Till it breaks on the shore of souls,—
            Alleluia!

On Heaven's transplendent shore,
  Where the great and mystic throng
Of crownèd saints now tune their harps
  To the everlasting song,—
            Alleluia!

That *song* no man may learn,
  Save earth's redeem'd and crown'd,
With "Harpers harping with their harps,"
  And silver trumpets' sound,—
            Alleluia!

Before the Lamb they kneel,
      By the " great white throne" they stand
In shining robes of righteousness,
      With palms in each outstretch'd hand—
                  Alleluia !

THE SONG.

Rev. xv. 3.

GREAT and marvellous are thy works,
      Lord God Almighty—just and true
In all thy ways, O King of Saints,
      Morning and evening, ever new !

Who shall not fear Thee, mighty Lord,
      And glorify Thy wondrous name ?
O Holy, Holy, Lord of Hosts,
      Through all eternity the same—
                  Alleluia, Amen !

O Alleluia grand !
      " Let earth keep silence," when
The courts of Heaven hush their praise
      To that sublime " Amen."

For silver trumpets call
  And myriad golden strings ;
While seraphs veil their faces in
  The silence of their wings.

O wave of wondrous might !
  O soundless depths of praise !
O earthly anthems ! faint your type
  Of those the ransomed raise !

Let Alleluias ring !
  Faint echoes from that shore
May teach us here that song to sing
  In Heaven for evermore.
                Amen.

AT JACQUELINE PASCAL'S GRAVE.

SLEEP on, sweet Saint, and take your rest
 In this green hallow'd shade,
Beneath the cross, the sacred sign,
 Among the blossoms laid.

Beneath the cross, so meekly borne,
 So lowly at His feet;
Till life thou didst not count too dear,
 To make thy death complete.

Faithful, so faithful to the last,
 Meek servant of the cross;
Who for one well belovèd Name,
 Counted all Earth's gain loss.

Plant laurel then, with lilies white,
 And "Sisters," here entwine
Sweet summer roses to adorn
 This gentle Saint's low shrine.

For now she lives beyond the stars,
   Life's battle boldly won ;
Above the cross she saw her crown
   Which 'mid all darkness shone.

Through cloister shades her upward path
   Led peaceful, calm, and blest,
'Twas through her cross *she* reach'd her crown.
   And enter'd into rest.

And this sweet burden all her life,
   The Cross, the Cross, she bore,
Till sinking from its weight at last,
   She reach'd the Golden Door.

´TIME'S SEA.

TIME'S sea rolls on o'er life's wild ebbing
  shore,
  Where wrecks and broken spars bestrew the
    strand;
Far, far we gaze beyond earth's misty main,
  Where Time's sea breaks upon another land.

Celestial waves! methinks I hear ye break
  In hushful whispers on that tuneful shore;
Chiming to one grand rhythm, one great verse—
  Eternity's full anthem, " Evermore !"

Here, wither'd hopes and broken shrines sleep
    low,
  Here faded garlands untwined, bloom to die,
Here buried in the drifts of shale and weed,
  The lone shell breathes her hollow minstrelsy.

There, crystal wavelets murmur peaceful rest,
    Immortal garlands breathe no more decay;
There, footsteps in the golden sands but track
    Earth's happy wanderers in their new array.

Now spirits glorified, redeemed, and freed
    From sorrow, sickness, and temptation's power;
Who've wash'd their spotless robes in blood of Him
    Whose lives were bought by His in earth's brief
        hour.

Where walls of jasper shut the holy in,
    And chrysolite and beryl flash their light;
Where every gate a single pearl doth shine,
    And where the nations saved now " walk in
        white."

There wander they in robes of spotless white,
    Among the many mansions of the blest,
There walk they in those "golden streets" of Life,
    There live they on, in love and changeless rest.

Where neither sun nor moon nor planet's rays
    Shall ever needed be in that great light;
And where the night shall no more dim the day,
    And where the gates are never shut at night.

And where the sun shall never more go down,
　And Christ shall wipe all tears of earth away;
And sin no more shall weave her death-shroud o'er
　The one eternal and transplendent day.

Beside that mighty " River's" crystal depths,
　Beneath the fragrant shade of that great tree;
The " tree of life" whose bending branches bear
　The glowing fruits of Immortality,

Calm rest they with their golden harps re-strung,
　And little children too of earth's brief day,
Who never knew our schools of error, guilt,
　But in their sinless season pass'd away.

There play they now with roses, lilies fair,
　And pluck sweet fruits that know no worm at
　　core;
Where no remember'd sins can ever blight
　Their perfect happiness for evermore.

And there the loving and the loved at length
　Shall never know one pang, one doubt, one pain,
But hand in hand shall wander evermore
　And parting never, never know again.

A PARAPHRASE

ON THE THIRTEENTH CHAPTER OF CORINTHIANS.

THOUGH I speak with the tongues of men,
　　Of angels pure and great;
And have not the gift of charity,
　　My words evaporate.

Like the clanging sound of brass,
　　Or the cymbal's tinkling ire,
All eloquence of earth is mute,
　　Save charity inspire.

Yet if the gift of prophecy
　　Were e'en vouchsafed to me,
With power to solve and analyse
　　All knowledge—mystery;

And though I had all steadfast faith,
　　The mountains to remove;
And had not the gift of charity,
　　The Heavenly gift of Love;

And though my goods I all bestow,
 To feed and clothe the poor ;
And give my body to be burn'd,
 It profiteth no more,

If love within my heart be dead,
 There hard, unkind, and cold,
Severe, detracting, envious,
 And slow to praise or hold

The good I in my neighbour see,
 The good in him I know—
All my best works drop down to dust,
 And I for darkness sow.

Ay ! though I seem a saint in white,
 And have not charity,
Like a dead corpse without the life,
 My master judgeth me.

For charity doth suffer long,
 For charity is kind,
For charity to failings, faults
 Of others, must be blind.

O sweetest grace of charity !
  O Godlike gift of love !
Transforming e'en the features to
  The angel-type above.

Nor envieth she, nor vaunteth e'er
  Herself to other's eyes,
Nor in her intercourse is harsh,
  But gentle, loving, wise ;

As hides the ragged rents, and crowns
  The ivy evergreen,
So charity must grow from roots
  In Paradise, I ween.

Not easily provoked is she,
  And evil thinketh none,
Suspicion clouds not her sweet face,
  But love is stamp'd thereon.

She mourneth o'er iniquity,
  Rejoiceth in the truth ;
Beareth all things patiently,
  And keeps the grace of youth.

This love then never faileth us,
  But prophecies shall fail,
And tongues shall lose their eloquence,
  When death shall life assail.

But here abideth Faith and Hope,
  Love—godlike Trinity;
But the greatest gift and grace of all,
  My child, is Charity.

"HE LEADETH THEM."

To A. B. L. G.

" And now beside thee, bleating lamb,
  I can lie down and sleep,
Or think on Him who bore thy name,
  Graze after thee and weep."
                    WILLIAM BLAKE.

HE leadeth them, He leadeth them
    Beside still waters' flow,
He resteth them, and feedeth them
    Where greenest pastures grow.

O'er stony steeps, o'er grassless plains,
    O'er 'wildering crags, through heat,
And cold, and storm, and beating rains,
    He finds paths for their feet.

The lambs He in His bosom bears,
    In shelter safe and warm,
And gently leads the wanderers
    Back to the fold from harm.

Thus, dearest Shepherd of Thy fold,
   Lead *us* to waters still ;
Nor let our wayward fancies bold,
   Seek self without, or will.

From Thine own Shrine to sheltering palms,
   O guide our wandering feet,
Till, folded in the eternal calms,
   We rest from earth's short beat.

How faithless we who bear Thy name,
   How faltering each step,
Although Thine own—the path the same
   We follow, Lord, but weep.

TRANSPOSITIONS.

SONNET OF MICHELANGELO.

NOR hath the mighty artist one conceit,
    That is not in the marble block en-
        shrined,
And only he may hope success to meet,
Who makes his work obedient to his mind.
The ill I flee, the good that I would fain
Centre in thee, fair lady, goddess proud,
There hides itself, and whilst I live, in vain
My art would war on longings, trebly vow'd;
Love here has wrought not e'en thy beauty great,
Nor fortune, coldness, nor supreme disdain,
For my great fault, or destiny, or fate,
But if within thy heart lives pity's strain,
Although but powerless to win thy love,
There still remains but Death's faint sweets to
    prove.

SONNET.

OF LAURA BATTIFERRO.

(1560).

THUS as a pitying father sees his son,
   Wandering afar in error's fatal snares,
And turning from the right path unawares,
In which so long he train'd his feet to run,
And still with face benign, and spirit mild,
He threatens not, nor blames, but hourly prays
For the return to truth and happier ways,
Of this his wayward and rebellious child.
So, O great God, more partial far than he,
Art Thou to this thy erring daughter, though
Stamp'd in Thy image but a wanderer too,
Yet now my soul returns all lovingly,
In sweet repentance yearning yet to be
Drawn by Thy love e'en closer still to Thee.

SONNET.

OF MM. MORELLI FERNANDEZ (FRA GLI ARCADI)

CORILLA OLIMPICA.

POETESSA LAUREATA IN CAMPIDOGLIO.

(1775).

NO fond conceit nor false ambition vain,
　　Allured me here—Imperial Rome, I come
To muse upon thy trophies' countless sum,
In guardianship of Time's edacious reign.
And as a torch illumes the sacred cave,
Spinning from dense and blackest night the light,
So is my silent soul subdued at sight
Of thee, grows eloquent, and strong, and brave;
Arcadia's forests long beguiled my feet,
Sacred to Phœbus, muses, sylvan gods,
To worship wisdom in the silent woods;
Now fortune smiles on me with honours great,
If her rewards I've toil'd for honestly,
Let none my laurel crown usurp from me.

SONNET.

ATTRIBUTED TO PETRARCH,

(FOUND IN THE TOMB OF MADONNA LAURA IN AVIGNON.)

1558.

ERE lie the chaste remains and cherish'd
  bones
Of that sweet spirit, rarest soul on earth,
Buried beneath these cold remorseless stones,
Are honour, fame, and beauty's matchless worth,
Death the green laurel now hath cut and torn,
Each tender root, and my poor warfare's o'er ;
Four " lustres " once beamed o'er me ; now forlorn
The spectral glooms descend ; to rise no more !
O happy plant in shades of Avignon,
That bloom'd and died ! Alas ! with thee must lie
The poet's pen and pencil—Genius gone.
O lovely body, living torch ! O why
Hast still no power to warm ? I bend my knee,
And pray to God His love hath welcomed thee.

A PARAPHRASE ON HEINE.

LAY thy hand, Dear, on my heart,
Dost hear it in its chamber beat?
For there a secret carpenter
Is making me my coffin neat.

There hammers he all night and day,
From happy sleep my eyes to keep,
Make haste then, master carpenter,
For I am ready now to sleep.

LATIN PRAYER OF MARY, QUEEN OF SCOTS.

H Lord my God, I hope in Thee!
O Jesu mine, deliver me!
In heavy chains, in weary pains,
Thus longing I desire but Thee,

Fainting ever, groaning ever,
Lord, to Thee I bend the knee,
While adoring, while imploring,
That Thou wouldst deliver me.

" O QUOT UNDIS LACRYMARUM."

WHAT waves of tears are rolling !
O what anguish never known !
Lo ! the Virgin, and reposing
In her arms her bleeding One—
From the blood-stain'd cross descended,
See the Blessed Virgin's son.

O that face, that form so lovely !
O that sweetest side where beat
Once the sacred heart of Jesus !
Wash, O tears, those bloodstain'd feet !
O those hands, transfix'd and bleeding,
Blessed hands, so pale and sweet !

Countless times she clasps the body,
   Countless kisses press each wound,
All her soul is steep'd in anguish,
   Here love's faithfulness is found—
Till that tender form exhausted,
   Drooping faints in woe profound.

Blessed Mary, we invoke thee
   By those tears o'er Jesus wept,
By those purple wounds all bleeding,
   By the grief thou didst accept,
May we share thy grief and sorrow,
   May we weep as thou hast wept!

A VESPER HYMN TO ST. MONICA.

" Ave dies lætitiae."

AIL! bright day of joy and gladness,
   Day of days, refulgent, great;
Which the Church appoints, rejoicing,
   And loving, we commemorate.

T

Brightly glows the Altar's splendour
  On the Faithful lowly bent,
Who swell with joy th' exultant chorus
  To Monica the holy saint.

Of virgins chaste this saint was chastest,
  Of marriage too, a mirror fair;
Of widows was the purest widow,
  Of each three au example rare.

O saintly one in thy sad weeping,
  A seed didst sow in every tear,
To exultant spring—returning
  On the Church new every year.

Holy Saint! we thus invoke thee,
  Thy maternal heart to move,
By the " Holy Three" protect us,
  Intercede for us above.

A PARAPHRASE ON ST. AUGUSTINE.

UT dust and ashes are we, Lord,
 Yet Thou hast deign'd to throw
Thine eyes of pity on this dust,
 Thus endless love to show.

Ay, on this dust Thine eyes have look'd,
 The clay in mould then laid
With tenderest pity,—Lo! a vase,
 For glory Thou hast made;

And gilded it with dropping rays
 From Thine own fingers bright;
And in this golden vase hast hid
 Thine own immortal light.

Charging Thine Angels from above,
 To keep it safe below;
Bidding them e'er defend Thy vase,
 From sin's sad overthrow.

A HYMN TO THE SAINTS IN HEAVEN.

(A Paraphrase on St. Augustine.)

OH ! stars of glory, lights of Heaven !
 Shed down on me your mystic light ;
Illume the storms that round me threaten,
 Reveal the perils of the night

Through which my barque of life is steering,
 So frail—to pirates oft exposed ;
Guard it from rocks and reefs of peril,
 Till in the eternal port enclosed,

The little freight is moor'd in safety,
 Which I have tried to garner here
In commerce spiritual, hoping
 It yet may reach the haven dear.

Then stars of glory, lights of Heaven,
 Shed down on me your mystic light,
Guide me, O guide me to the haven
 Where Faith is swallow'd up in Sight.

" MIS DESIOS."

(FROM THE SPANISH OF D. JUAN BAUTISTA DE ARRIAZA.)

F God should on me one great gift confer,
    Of all I might receive, and He bestow,
Nor gold, nor silver, would I then prefer,
    Nor empires, crowns, nor earthly fame below.
Or if one talent were vouchsafed to me,
    'Twere happiness I would elect as chief;
For e'en the sages proved all vanity,
    All science incomplete for life so brief.
Thus only one great boon I'd ask from Heaven,
    One gift of happiness conceded here,
And which would crown my earthly peace if
        given—
    Namely, one faithful friend for life, for e'er,
One true and noble heart, and only one—
    I have that friend—that friend hath led me on !